THE STONE

DOORWAY

BY CASSANDRA SCHERER

Line By Lion Publications
5916 Ashby Ln.
Louisville, KY 40272
www.linebylion.com

ISBN: 978-1-940938-46-2

CHAPTER ONE

On the day that Tori McKenna's life became surprisingly unordinary, she had observed how painfully normal she had let her existence become. A thought she would later regret. It started off in its normal, simple fashion; eating breakfast in the kitchen alone while panicked about the day ahead. She walked to school alone, threatened by the very glance of other classmates. School dragged by in its ordinary fashion with Tori silently existing in the back rows of classrooms and making herself as small as possible in the hallways, bleeding right into track practice. This, for Tori, was the best part of her day. The slap of her sneakers against the surface of the track, the wind blowing her chestnut hair and the warm sun beating down on her bare shoulders melted away the stress and panic of the day and made her feel more alive than she had in 2 years. The sensation always died away too quickly afterward, but she came back every day to get a taste of what "living" felt like.

On this particular day, her walk home veered off from normalcy when she heard the horn beep in that annoying "shave and a haircut, two bits" rhythm. Her blood chilled as she turned and saw the late '80s Chevy, suped up beyond belief, the details to which were burned into her memory. Her heart rate quickened and she felt the familiar fear of the driver rising up, threatening to strangle her.

"What do you want?" She wouldn't look directly at him through the opened passenger window. She couldn't. "You're not supposed to be within 500 feet of me," she tried so hard to sound firm, but she could hear the tremble in her voice.

"Not as of eight am this morning," Beau Shaw smiled at her across the cab of the truck. He was unquestionably handsome, standing 6'1" with short strawberry blonde patch atop his head; he was a catch to some. Not to mention he could easily bench press two of Tori. These were many of the reasons Tori had swooned when he passed her in the hallways of school and had squealed with delight when they had started dating her sophomore year. They had been the all American, picture perfect couple. She had been the envy of every girl. Their eyes had followed her down every hallway; she remembered feeling pride at the jealousy she managed to elicit from the other girls. That is, until Beau's anger and fists emerged. The first two times he hit her, she hid it from everyone with make-up and lame excuses. He would apologize with beautiful and extravagant flower arrangements. He would pamper her for weeks and eventually the memory of the injury would fade. The third time she was unable hide it, ending not only their relationship but also his football scholarship to college, something for which he placed the blame solely on Tori. Since the restraining order he'd stayed away…. Until today.

"Lemme give you a ride home."

"What?! No! Go away!" Tori turned and continued her walk down the sidewalk, watching the blue truck roll alongside her in her peripheral. After a few feet she turned and faced him, "What?!"

"Come on….," he coaxed, "Take a ride with me baby." He put the truck in park but before Beau could lift the lever to open his door Tori turned and bolted down the sidewalk, heart hammering in her chest. From behind her she heard the door squeak open and slam shut again as Beau gave chase. His footfalls were loud and coming at an incredible speed. Tori's panic was working against her, he was catching her fast. She rounded the corner at the end of the block, cutting across a neatly manicured lawn with Beau only steps behind her. She dared a glance over her shoulder to see how close he was when a lip in the sidewalk grabbed her toe. She tried to correct herself but her purse strap tangled around her forearm, inhibiting her from righting herself and down she went. Pain rocketed through her wrist like an explosion and she felt the skin tear away from her knee. She turned over desperately pawing through her purse for her pepper spray. Beau laughed, red faced and winded, he still found humor in her attempts at courage.

"Oh, so NOW you get brave? Pathetic little girl." With his full momentum behind him he balled a fist and punched Tori knocking her backward onto the sidewalk. Stars danced in her vision. She lifted her head from the sidewalk trying desperately to remain conscious as Beau towered over her. Before Tori could put a hand up to block the next blow, a blur came from her right and suddenly Beau was gone. Tori looked around confused, head bobbing and weaving, vision still blurry trying to figure out what had just happened.

Tori! Get it together!

She shook her head then rose to her hands and knees, which hurt, but the tussle taking place on the beautifully manicured lawn to her left made her forget the pain. Beau and a black haired boy were rolling around on the grass. And, although the dark haired boy was quite a bit smaller, he was quick and rapidly getting the best of Beau. The Dark Hair Boy threw himself on top of Beau's chest and pinned his arms to ground on either side of his head.

"Enough!" The Dark Haired Boy yelled. "We're done," Beau struggled for a minute then settled, giving in.

"For now Pretty Boy," Beau rasped.

The Dark Haired Boy rose from the grass, leaving Beau to his defeat.

"Hey…. It's okay. Are you all right?" The Dark Haired Boy, barely panting, reached his hand down to Tori. His voice was sweet and he didn't seem to be mocking her like Beau used to after he'd hit her. He was helping her. She took his hand gingerly and stood, a little dizzy but it passed quickly and she regained her composure. She finally looked the boy in the face and he was…. well, gorgeous. He had jet black hair that fell above his ears and olive skin. But his eyes.

Oh my god, his eyes are beautiful.

His emerald eyes were perfectly framed by long black lashes that made them look even more like gem stones. Tori looked away self-consciously.

"I need to call the cops" she said shakily

"Okay, I'll find a phone"

The nice old lady, on whose sidewalk Tori had tripped, allowed them to call the police, who were all too happy to drag Beau to jail. Gorgeous Eyes never left her side.

After the cops left and the street quieted again, Tori grew anxious and broke the silence.

"Thank you for stepping in, you really didn't have to." She sounded so small.

"You don't need to thank me. You were in trouble, I just happened to come by at the right time." He paused, "I'm Dean by the way."

"I'm Tori." She shook his hand awkwardly. She noticed a spot of blood near the corner of his mouth, without thinking she reached us and wiped the blood away with her sleeve. She immediately blushed. He smiled.

Nice smile too.

"Is that short for something?"

"Victoria, but everyone calls me Tori." She smiled at him again. "Well thank you again, but I need to get home." Tori turned to continue down the sidewalk when Dean stopped her.

"Hey, let me give you a ride." He gestured to a newer black trailblazer parked haphazardly on the side of the road. "I'm heading that way anyway. Besides, look at your knee."

Tori looked down; it did look a little nasty. But still she hesitated. She didn't know this boy at ALL and after what had just happened she didn't know if she should be accepting rides from dark haired strangers. No matter how attractive. Dean sensed her hesitation.

"You can stay unbuckled with the door open; anything creepy happens you can bail anytime." Tori smiled at this and nodded in acceptance.

"All right, thank you again."

They drove in silence for the few blocks to Tori's

house, the air thick with questions Tori wanted to ask him. Dean pulled into Tori's driveway and neither moved or said anything for a moment.

"So…. Who was that guy?" Dean finally asked.

"He….," Tori sighed heavily, "he is my psycho ex-boyfriend." Tori held her wrist and looked down at her bloodied knee. "It's so embarrassing." Tori put her face in her hands.

"No… Hey, listen to me." Dean gently took her chin and turned her head towards him. "You have nothing to be embarrassed about. That dude is CRAZY! At least you were smart enough not to get in the car with him." He took his hand away and looked out the window. "Some girls aren't so lucky." Tori didn't say anything but waited for him to continue. "My sister, Danielle, dated low life like that. One day, he picked her up for a date and she never came home. You were smart, Tori."

"I'm so sorry, Dean," Tori reached across the center console and took his hand; his skin was warm against hers. He smiled appreciatively.

"It's okay, thanks. We just moved right down there." He pointed down the block, "New start or something…. Anyway… Just my parents and I now."

"I should go," Tori smiled, "Thank you again" She reached down absentmindedly to gather her things when she realized they weren't there. She dropped her face in her hands, "Oh my god, I left my bag down the street." Tori leaned back in the seat and sighed. "I'm gonna walk back down and get my bag, thank you again... for everything." She opened the door and hopped out of the car.

"Wait a sec!" Dean called after her, "I'll go get it" Tori stared at him in astonishment.

"Really?"

"Yeah! You're leg's all torn up, I'll go get it and bring it back."

"No, seriously you don't have to do that. You've already done more than enough. Really."

"What kind of knight in shining armor would I be if I made you walk 3 blocks with a swollen wrist and scraped up knee to get your bag?" He flashed a perfect, sweet smile at her making her melt from the inside out. "Go inside, clean up that knee and I will be back in a second." He put the car in reverse and pulled back down her short driveway before she could protest. The stark contrast between how nice he was and how cruel Beau was startled her, he was too good to be true.

Tori watched the trailblazer head back down the street then gingerly walked up the sidewalk to her front door. She dug the hidden key out from the potted plant to the side of the door and let herself in to the empty house. Her mother was out of town again for some conference or another, and the quiet seemed to almost echo off the walls at her. She hated the silence of her empty house. After flipping on the radio near the front window, she fell into one of the arm chairs. The lace curtains hanging over the side windows filtered in the afternoon light, casting a warm glow over the room. The light danced off the pictures on the opposite wall. Embarrassing pictures of Tori dating back to preschool filled the wall, but there were none that she was truly smiling in. Not a single picture in her house that captured her being truly happy.

The rest of her house was quaint, filled with whitewashed country tables, doilies and table top knickknacks. The hardwood floors gleamed in the sunlight from around the several neatly placed throw rugs throughout the room. The stairs to her left ascended to the three bedrooms and large bathroom, ahead of her the living room opened up into a large kitchen with a door that opened up into a small, unkempt back yard, and another that led to a small bathroom. Tori stood and headed to the small bathroom to retrieve the first aid kit. She gathered the Band-Aids and peroxide and as an afterthought took the Ace bandage for her wrist as well, dumping all the supplies on the circular kitchen table. She sat down heavily with a sigh in one of the chairs and started to open the peroxide when she heard two quick knocks on the back door then a key disengaging a lock. She smiled at the sound.

"Hey Allen," she said as the backdoor opened and her lanky neighbor entered

"Hey T-bird how's it go…. What happened?" Allen dropped the keys on the table and immediately turned to the freezer for an ice pack. He crossed the kitchen quickly and put the ice on her face, then examined her knee and wrist. Allen and Tori had been friends since they'd been in diapers, they'd lived next door to one another their whole lives and for a while they had been each other's whole world. When Tori's dad left, Allen was there for Tori, and when Allen's mom got sick Tori went to the hospital with him. When Tori didn't think she had the strength to leave Beau, Allen gave her the tough love her mother was unable to give her. They had never tried to date, the fact was, she and Allen were so close the thought was weird to them. It wasn't that Allen wasn't handsome with his tall, slender build, warm brown eyes and sandy blonde hair that always seemed to fall perfectly into place no matter what he did. He WAS handsome…. But they had always needed each other as friends more than they had needed each other as lovers. So they became the siblings they never had, and often the only family either one ever had. Allen's dad had never been around and after his mom finally succumbed to the cancer he was alone. Tori's mom kept her mind and life busy to avoid feeling the loss of her husband, Tori's father, after he left with another woman. Tori's father had then died a few years later of liver failure, leaving her truly alone. "Spill it T. What happened?"

"Beau stopped me on the way home."

"What?! What about the restraining order?" Allen yelled nearly knocking the chair over as he jumped to his feet.

"The restraining order expired this morning. Will you sit down please? I hate it when you get all…. Stressie." Tori flipped her hand at him and after fuming a few more seconds he sat down. "Thank you," She sighed.

"Okay, so they what happened?" Allen said coolly.

"Beau pulled up in that stupid truck of his, he wanted to give me a ride or something. I wouldn't get in the car and he got mad so I ran… I tripped down the street and he was right on top of me… and he hit me." Tori looked down at the table, she felt so feeble and embarrassed. She was so sick of being afraid. Allen was fuming inside but he spoke calmly to her.

"T-bird, it's not your fault. That jerk has the problem, NOT you!" He reached across the table and put a hand on her forearm. "Did you call the cops?"

"Yeah, after…" Tori blushed and smiled despite herself.

"After what? What could possibly be funny?"

"Not funny." Tori tried to find the right words. "Sweet."

Allen stared at her blankly for several seconds.

"And this is why I am single. I don't get girls." Allen threw his hands up in exasperation. Tori laughed at his reaction. "Seriously T, the guy hits you and its SWEET?"

"No, not Beau!" Tori waved her hands in front of her clearing the confusion, "This guy, this gorgeous guy came out of nowhere and beat the shit out of Beau!"

"What?" Allen shook his head, "do you have a concussion?"

"No listen. This guy happened to be driving by and saw Beau attack me and he…. he saved me." She smiled and thought about the events for a moment then took the peroxide off the table and poured it on a nearby dishcloth and began cleaning her bleeding knee. "He's down the street where it happened getting my bag right now." Tori flinched at the stinging in her knee.

Allen was quiet a minute.

"Is this guy okay?" he finally asked.

"Allen...," Tori started.

"No, listen Tori. Your taste in men is...." He was obviously searching for the right words. "It sucks. Your taste in men sucks, T-bird. This guy could be another Beau, you know nothing about him."

"I know he isn't Beau." Tori motioned to the front windows where she could see the black trailblazer pulling back in the driveway, "See for yourself."

Allen stood and walked to the doorway between the two rooms and watched the black vehicle park. They both waited for the knock at the door, when it came and Tori moved to answer the door Allen rushed into the living room

"No, please let me," he smiled. Tori sighed and sat back down. "What's his name again? Lancelot?"

"Ha! Very funny!"

Allen answered the door and said nothing. An awkward tension started to build.

"Hey, is Tori here?" Dean's voice carried to the kitchen causing butterflies to flutter through Tori's stomach.

"Yeah." Allen was laying on his protective bravado thick. "And?"

"I have her bag.... Is this the right house? Is she here?" Dean didn't seem daunted at all, just confused.

"Who are you?"

"Don't worry about who I am," Tori began chewing her nails. Then Allen laughed, "Nah, I'm just messing with you. I'm Allen, Lancelot, come in."

The boys walked in, Allen smiling from the torture he had put Tori through. When Dean entered the kitchen, Tori suddenly became very aware of how she looked, and how out of place Dean looked in her home.

Oh my goodness, he's in my house!

"Hey, how's the cheek?" He cringed as he looked down at her leg, "And the knee?"

"Bruised and bloody," Tori smiled as she went back to cleaning her knee.

"Here's your bag," he said gently, setting it down on the floor next to her chair. He rounded the table to the chair closest to Tori and carefully took the towel from her. "You can't *wipe* it, dab it. You'll make it worse." Dean gently cleaned out her knee then bandaged the wound for her. When he was finished, Tori exhaled not realizing she had been holding her breath.

"So hero, what's your name? Or should I just keep calling you Lancelot?" Allen joked. Dean smiled pleasantly, obviously not threatened by Allen.

"Dean Cordilla. And you are… her brother?" Allen waved his hand and sat down across from Tori the at the table.

"Close enough, I live next door."

"Our moms were friends when we were growing up, his mom was awesome when my dad left," Tori filled in putting the ice pack back to her face.

"I'm sorry," Dean said genuinely.

"Thanks, it's okay. I hear he was a jerk." Tori laughed. She watched Dean carefully; his cheeks were seated high amidst his olive skin. His eyes held none of the dark, angry shadows that she used to see in Beau's eyes. Dean caught her starring and she instantly looked away, face burning with embarrassment.

"Okay well, it's getting a little too…. Whatever this is, for me." Allen stood and kissed Tori on the head. "I'll see you tonight T-bird."

"What's tonight?" Dean asked.

"There's a meteor shower tonight. It's supposed to be amazing. Allen and I were going to order bad food and watch the stars fall." Tori looked up at Allen, begging with her eyes to invite her rescuer. Allen sighed.

"Yeah, come by." Allen said, "I'm ordering pizza at 8:00." Allen opened the door but stopped halfway out and turned back to Tori. "Hey if Beau comes back, you call me. They might not hold him."

Tori threw a thumbs up over her shoulder as Allen shut and relocked the back door.

"So you guys are close, huh?" Dean asked.

"Yeah, he's my best friend. His mom died a couple years ago and now I'm really all he has. What about your family?"

"Well, we were the most normal family I knew until Danielle," he was quiet for a moment. "Now we are as normal as we can be." They stared at each other for a few minutes in silence. When Dean finally rose he said, "I gotta get home but, can I take you up on that offer? Pizza and star gazing?" Tori almost leapt out of her seat.

"Absolutely." She may have said a little too enthusiastically. She cleared her throat. "Yeah, sounds great. 8:00?"

"I'll be here." Dean leaned in and kissed her gently on her right cheek. Heat radiated through her body and goose bumps rippled down her arms. Dean turned and left Tori sitting in her kitchen, bandage knee, blackened eye and high as a kite.

CHAPTER TWO

Butterflies twisted in her stomach as the clocked neared 8 o'clock. Tori had managed to change into jeans without ripping off her knee bandage and she found a shirt that hung slightly loose upon her body. She fussed over her hair and tried two more shirts before limping down the stairs to wait for Dean. Allen got there first, of course, and let himself in by the back door, arms full of pizza boxes and 2 liters of soda.

"Hero Boy get here yet?"

"Not yet," Tori took the 2 liters from his arms and cleared space in the fridge for them while Allen cleared the table and set down the pizza.

"Well he has to be a little late so he doesn't look too eager," Allen joked, but Tori turned and glared at him as she looked up at the clock again. "Relax, he'll be here." As if on cue, headlights shined through the front windows lighting up the back kitchen wall. "See! Do you want me to get it?"

Tori chewed her nail and worked at the meat on the side of her finger as she looked toward the front door, a nervous habit she'd had since she was small. She was so nervous.

When am I not nervous?

"Ugh… I'll get it!" Allen sighed.

"NO!" Tori jumped in front of him. "I'll get it."

She started through the living room towards the door but turned back towards Allen. "Just be cool okay? No more macho crap." Allen smiled and made a halo over his head with his fingers.

Tori opened the door as Dean was walking up the front steps, flowers in hand.

Tori's breath caught in her throat as the world stood perfectly still for a moment as they stared at each other. The porch lights shined off his dark hair and made his green eyes light up. He was the first to break the silence.

"You look beautiful," He crossed the small porch and put a soft hand on her bruised cheek. He brought the flowers up to her and smiled.

"You brought me flowers?"

"No they're for Allen." Dean laughed and handed her bouquet. "Of course I brought you flowers," he said in a low and sweet tone. Tori grinned and stepped aside.

"Come in."

After the pizza was eaten, Dean helped clear the dishes from the table as Allen and Tori cleaned the rest of the dinner remnants from the kitchen.

"So where's your mom anyway?" Dean asked as he spilled the uneaten crusts into the trash can.

"Conference in Chicago." Tori handed the remaining half a two liter to Allen who stood with the fridge door open rearranging condiments to fit the leftover pizza and soda. Tori's wrist still throbbed and it looked like the swelling had only gotten worse as the ace bandage was exponentially tighter than it was an hour ago. Allen closed the door to the fridge and nodded toward her wrist.

"I've got an old splint at my house. I can go get it for you, T." He grabbed the empty pizza boxes and headed out the back door.

"He seems to really care about you," Dean said from the sink.

"Yeah, he does. But it's not like that. He works and goes to college but I think he just gets lonely. Plus being in that house is like living with a ghost." Tori made her way to the sink and began rinsing the plates.

"Yeah, I get that. We moved 1,000 miles to get away from our ghost."

"He's here a lot, which is fine because I'm alone a lot…. Look at that!" Tori shouted, dropping a plate into the sink and making Dean jump.

"What?!"

"Look at all the stars!" Even with the light of the kitchen at their backs the falling meteors were blazing bright. "There must be a million of them. And look at that one, it's almost blue!"

"Whoa! Look at that one!" Dean leaned across the kitchen sink and angled his head out the window. "It's BIG. Is it getting closer?"

"What? No way." Tori leaned closer to the window as well in disbelief but as she did so she saw a bright, blue ball of light growing larger as it closed in on Earth. The sky began to brighten as the object grew and got closer, until the entire sky bright blue. The kitchen lights blinked spastically then died, the room filled with the eerie blue light.

"Oh my god, it's going to hit us!" The meteor grew huge as it descended on to Tori's house, the room began to grow brighter and brighter. Tori and Dean shielded their eyes from the intrusive light, crouching behind the counter. Suddenly the room began to vibrate, the floor rumbling underneath them. It was soft at first but grew quickly into a roar of quaking walls. Glasses, dishes and knickknacks crashed to the floor, shattering into a thousand pieces, Dean covered Tori with his upper body to shield her as a kitchen chair toppled against the counter above them.

The ear deafening roar drowned out the sound of the breaking glass and falling furniture but they both looked up as the back door flew open and a terrified Allen threw himself into the kitchen. He frantically crawled across the kitchen floor over the broken glass, batting the chair out of his way. He crouched, on the floor next to Tori and Dean. The blinding light filled the room, piercing their eyes and the horrible, ear splitting roar pressed until it felt as if their ears might rupture, the windows above the sink burst against the pressure of the sound. Then…

BOOM!

And then silence.

CHAPTER THREE

The lights flickered back on as the three still cowered on the floor, faces hidden and hands pressed to their ears. Slivers of glass covered them from the window above the sink. Tori looked around the kitchen, which was in shambles. They all sat up slowly, letting the glass slide off of them.

"You guys okay?" Dean asked.

"What was that?" Allen asked as he stood.

"There's no way that thing actually fell here," Tori said as she stood with Allen and Dean's help "Right?" She wasn't so sure and she didn't think the guys were either.

Allen made his way across the kitchen, stumbling over furniture and dishes, and opened the back door.

"Oh my god……," he whispered. The light casting through the back door turned Allen's face blue.

"What is it?" Tori said sounding small, even to her own ears. Instead of answering he motioned for them to come over to him, silently. Dean and Tori carefully made their way to the open back door, their feet skidding on broken plates and glassware. Tori tripped on the fallen remains of one of the kitchen chairs but Dean caught her before she fell.

That's twice today he's saved me.

Allen moved aside to let them into the doorway,

and as Tori wrapped around the threshold she saw it....

Shining from the depths of the tall grasses and underbrush, a sphere of blue light lay about 200 yards beyond Tori's back fence.

"What is that?"

Without answering Allen grabbed Tori's hoodie off the flooring shaking off the broken glass, he threw it to her.

"We're going to find out."

"Flashlights?" Dean asked also in motion now, grabbing his own jacket from under a kitchen chair.

"Top drawer," Allen answered.

Tori shoved the hoodie over her head and watched as the boys collected flashlights, testing them all and shoving extra batteries hurriedly in their pockets.

"Wait... What are we doing? Should we even go out there?" Tori asked "Could it be dangerous or, I don't know, radioactive?"

"We've gotta check it out T-bird," Allen said stepping out on to the back steps. Dean handed Tori a flashlight and smiled as he touched her arm reassuringly.

"It's okay. We'll be fine." He shrugged on his coat then headed out into the night after Allen.

"Yay.... An adventure," Tori sighed as she reluctantly followed the guys into the yard. Allen had to force the rusted gate open but it finally gave. With a *creeeeeeeeeeeeeeek,* the gate opened to an overgrown path that led back to the field of sparse trees and scrub oak. The grass and cat tails were taller than Tori in some spots and the scrub oak grabbed at her clothes as they pushed their way down the trail.

As they neared the object, they didn't even need the flashlights, the blue light rode on a weird mist that had formed and swirled around them. Light wasn't a problem. The air was also thick with a sulfur smell that burned Tori's nostrils and stung her eyes. Allen coughed ahead of her against the stench and Dean rubbed at his face with his arm before reaching back and taking her hand. The action was so natural, so protective and sweet that the tingly butterfly feeling rippled through her again. But her bliss was short lived.

The light grew steadily brighter the closer they got to the sphere, as did the fog which began to take on a greyish blue color. The smell was becoming overwhelming as well; Tori put her sleeve over her mouth trying to avoid inhaling the noxious odor.

The grass and foliage finally gave way to a burnt clearing of scorched trees and underbrush. The clearing was a fifty foot circle, like the aftermath of an explosion, with a small pond sitting just right of center. Tori knew this pond well, she and Allen used to play here as kids, but this was not the scene she remembered from childhood. This was horrific. She felt her panic rising, but took a breath of thick, putrid air to calm herself.

Don't lose it, Tori!

"There!" Dean was pointing to the far side of the pond where a thick blue haze hung in circles around a blue stone jutting out from surface of the pond. The water near the stone actually boiled from the heat of the object. The ghostly fingers of the mist reached across the water, slithering across the surface.

"Come on," Allen urged, moving off the trail, around the right shore of the pond to where the stone rested, half in and half out of the water. The three stared in horror at it. "Look at the water. Look at the fish!" Fish of several different sizes floated belly up in the boiling water.

"Guys…. The fog," Tori said shakily. The blue mist was surrounding them now sifting through the air and remaining grass. They watched as it slithered from the huge stone to her feet, "Guys?" The smoky strands of mist wrapped themselves around their legs and torsos and finally bore itself into their eyes. As the mist moved between their eyelids it neither stung nor gave any other signs of its presence but it swirled behind their irises and altered all their eyes to grey.

"I feel weird," Tori mumbled feeling suddenly dizzy. Her vision darkened. Allen was shaking his head and Dean had his eyes closed pinching the bridge of his nose.

"Me too," Dean slurred.

"I want to touch it," Allen said, almost to himself. Tori and Dean looked at each other.

"What?" They said together.

"I said we need to move it." Allen looked at them confused, as if they hadn't been listening. "Look what it's doing to the water; we shouldn't leave it like that."

"Yeah, look what it's doing to the water Allen! That's why we shouldn't go near it!" Tori's head spun again making her woozy.

"You okay T?" Allen asked her, putting a hand on her elbow to steady her.

"Yes, I'm fine." Tori shook her head to clear it, "I want to go home, Allen."

"I'm with her, if it's killing the fish then it's toxic and I don't want anything to do with it," Dean agreed stepping closer to Tori and Allen.

Suddenly something grabbed him from the inside out. He fell instantly to his knees, hands to his eyes screaming in pain. The stone at the edge of the pond began pulsating brighter and brighter with intense blue light. As the pulsations grew more rapid Dean's screams grew louder and more frantic.

"Allen! Do something!" Tori screamed. Allen

moved to help Dean when suddenly he was seized by the same internal death grip. His knees bent forward, his torso bent back at the waist in a horrible seizure of pain until he finally fell to the ground. Allen's hands clamped over his ears as he too began to scream. The pulsating quickened as Tori ran for the boys crumpled a few feet from her when suddenly something grabbed her by the ankle sending her falling heavily to the ground. She desperately turned over, kicking at whatever had her left ankle.

What had her was a hand.

The hand was bloody.

And belonged to a child.

The boy stared at her with grey eyes that were far too old to be his. His tiny, emaciated body was covered in bruises and dried blood. His bone-thin fingers snaked around her ankle, trying to pull her towards him. He opened his mouth and as the sounds of the chaos around her faded away and silence closed in around her the boy whispered one word:

"Caligo"

Tori began screaming frantically as her heart hammered in her chest. She back pedaled on all fours away from the boy, clawing at the dirt, trying to twist away. Hands tightened around her arms pulling her upward and she desperately batted at them, reeling herself into a full scale panic. Tears streamed down her face, her throat grew raw from the screams still ripping from her.

"Tori!"

"Tori! Stop!" The fog and the panic both subsided and her vision cleared as Dean and Allen came into focus. She looked around wildly for the boy but the field was empty, save for the three of them.

"What the hell was that?" Tori whispered

"Are you okay?" Dean asked still holding her by the arm

"Yeah, but Allen. Please, we need to go," Tori pleaded.

"We need to get outta here," Dean agreed.

"Yeah, you're right. Let's get out of here and….." Allen stopped, a confused looked on his face. He was being dragged by an invisible thread toward the blue, pulsating stone. "What the…." Allen struggled against the unseen force. His feet sliding across the charred ground as he fought with all his strength.

"It's got him!" Dean shouted as he ran forward and grabbed Allen's arms, pulling back against the invisible tether.

"Allen!" Tori screamed as the invisible line pulling Allen snapped him backwards against the stone as if magnetized. Dean was still gripping Allen's forearms desperately trying to pry him from the stone as Allen started shrieking in fear. Dean put his foot up on the stone trying to push off for extra leverage.

At the sound of Allen's panic, Tori ran and grabbed Allen's arm. As her fingertips made contact with Allen's palm, she felt electricity surge through her body. The surge ignited a release of blinding, blue light from the stone. Tori tried to let go of Allen's hand and flee but she was fused to him and him to the stone. Tori's hand burned against Allen's. She closed her eyes against the light but the blue light seared through her eyelids, slicing into her brain with red hot pain. The sounds of Allen's screams were soon drowned out by her own. Scarlet pain soon eclipsed the blue light of the stone and just before the world faded to black, Tori saw the boy who had grabbed her ankle with the grey, all-consuming eyes.

He also began to scream.

CHAPTER THREE

Waking.

Howling.

Why was there howling?

Tori's head hurt so much, she moaned as she rolled onto her side. Doing so released the pressure of something hard stabbing her in the shoulder blade. Her face rested against what felt like grass, it poked at her cheek and made her itch.

"Tori? Where are you?" Allen's voice was low and husky like he was just waking as well.

"A…Allen. I'm here," Tori managed weakly. Her eyes stung from the bright light she blinked against the assault finally focusing on Allen who was a few feet away fumbling to his feet. As he eyes adjusted he slowly started to survey their strange new surroundings. Towering over them a few feet away was a huge boulder. It stood at least ten feet high and thick and ancient. On the side facing Tori, she could see letters etched into the surface of the stone spelling out the word 'Portis'. Beyond the stone, a valley stretched out around them blending easily to a mountain and thick forests spilling all around them.

And then she saw the source of the howling. A group of riders atop massive grey wolves stampeded toward them down the mountainside.

"Allen?" Tori quaked.

"They don't look friendly. Tori, we gotta go." Allen pulled her to her feet and began pulling her towards the closest outcropping of forest.

"Wait! Where's Dean?" Tori screamed, searching the ground frantically for him.

"Dean?!" Allen yelled spinning wildly looking for him. "Tori, there's someone here." Tori stopped screaming and turned to see two hooded figures emerging from the shadows of the forest. They seemed to hesitate when they saw the riders on wolf-back heading across the valley, but suddenly bolted from the forest the fifty or so yards to them. Tori stepped behind Allen but looked over her shoulder at the approaching danger descending the hillside. The cloaked people arrived quickly, one was quite a bit taller than the other, when the shorter of the two spoke, Tori knew why…. She was a girl. A girl with a faint English accent.

"You need to come with us. There's not much time," she said quickly.

"Who are you?" Allen demanded, "And where are we?" Tori glanced nervously over her shoulder at the riders who grew ever closer.

Cloaked English girl or menacing monster on a wolf? Yeah… decision made.

"Allen let's go," Tori pushed past Allen grabbing

his arm and dragging him along. "Wherever they take us will be better than where THEY," Tori turned Allen and pointed toward the herd of riders barreling down on them, "plan on taking us". She turned back to the girl, "There was another guy with us."

"We've already got him. Follow us and stay close." With a swish of her cloak they were running, with Allen and Tori close behind. The sounds of the riders grew louder and louder, she could hear the wolves breathing now.

We're never going to make it.

Tori dared a glance back over her shoulder and when she did a rock caught her foot, cranking her ankle to the side. She went down hard, pain shooting up her leg. She tried to scramble back to her feet but her ankle protested and she went down again. Allen and the girl were almost to the woods.

"HELP!" Tori screamed, clawing at the ground toward the tree line. Suddenly, the larger of the two escorts burst from the trees running at an intense rate. He got to her in mere seconds, scooping her up in his arms as he turned back toward the forest. An arrow whizzed by his head, Tori screamed and buried her head in his chest. Eyes closed against reality. Tori could hear the grind of claws into earth, straps hitting hide, metal bridals clanging, all within feet of them now. Another arrow flew past them skimming her leg, ripping only her jeans.

Then they were in the cover of the trees. He set her carefully, yet quickly on the ground as if she weighed nothing. Tori watched in horror as the riders closed the last few feet between them. The boy grabbed Tori by the waist and stuffed her into a crevice between a huge boulder and the earth where Allen and the girl waited. Once inside he muscled another boulder over the opening, sealing them in.

The closeness was suffocating but the enemies outside were far scarier. The sound of all of their breathing echoed off the walls of their stone hideaway, but over that Tori could hear the riders outside. They stopped at the edge of the forest, Tori guessed the trees were too dense for their gigantic mounts, but a couple men came in on foot. Their heavy footfalls and clanking armor paused momentarily outside the small cave, the four held their breath. Tori closed her eyes and laid her head against her knees, willing them to go away. After several agonizing minutes, they did just that.

"I KNOW YOU HAVE THE NEWLINGS, LITTLE GIRL!" A massive voice boomed through the forest, making Tori jump, "BUT NOT FOR LONG! I WILL HAVE THEM!" After a long pause, they heard the riders retreating across the valley again. Their footfalls and clanking armor growing further and further away. Tori's heart thundered in her ears, keeping time with the throbbing in her ankle.

For a long time, no one moved and no one spoke. Finally the girl exhaled and whispered, "That was close."

"Who are they?" Allen asked quietly.

"The Caligo. The tribe of raiders that lives up the mountain." The name set off a bell in Tori's head. The boy at the blue stone had said "Caligo," hadn't he? She said nothing.

"They've been getting here quicker and quicker every time," the boy said, as he shuffled past Tori, pushing the boulder away and peeking outside. "It's clear." He shoved the boulder aside the rest of the way and waved everyone out.

"What do you mean?" Allen asked as he made his way out of hiding.

"Whenever the Portis opens we try to get here before the scavs do. We don't want them to capture the newcomers like you. They are animals." The girls answered as she helped Tori to her feet... well foot.

"Wait, what?" Allen nearly rocked back off his feet. "What is going on?"

"We will explain more back at the village, but we really need to go." The girl ignored Allen's shock at the situation.

"Well, who are you?" Tori demanded. The girl nodded and took down her hood. She was beautiful. She had glistening pale blonde hair and brilliant blue eyes. Her porcelain skin was marred only but the grey that threatened to creep into her eyes. Like the boy from the field, her eyes were far too old to be hers.

"I'm Sari and this is Seth" When he unhooded himself, the similarities between them were striking. Besides the difference in size, they looked identical. They were twins. Seth's eyes were just as dazzling as his sister's and settled on Tori.

"I'm Allen, this is Tori. Our friend Dean was with us but you said…"

"He's already back at the village. He was badly injured when he came through the Portis. It took two of us to move him without doing more damage. We will take you to him."

Sari turned to head deeper into the forest.

"Wait, came through? Came through what? To Where?" Tori exclaimed.

"You three came through a doorway from your world to ours." Seth told her keeping his steady gaze.

"Your WORLD?!" Tori shouted, almost laughing.

"Seth we have to go," Sari urged but Seth continued.

"You saw a blue rock, yeah?" Tori and Allen

nodded "That stone is a doorway from your world to this one. You came in through that stone out there, the Portis."

"So where are we?" Tori suddenly felt the gravity of their situation settle upon her.

"We call it Everidge," Seth smiled. Tori's head spun. She leaned against the boulder hideout to steady herself.

"Who was the boy?" Tori finally asked.

"What boy?" Sari asked her.

"Right before we... came through... there was a boy. He couldn't have been more than 9 but he was all bloody and beaten but his eyes were... old... like yours."

Seth and Sari looked at one another.

"The Caligo must have had an escapee," Seth said to Sari. He regarded Tori again, "When the scavs are able to capture a newling, a new comer, they use them as slaves. And worse."

"But why would they use *children?*" Tori heard the tears in her voice.

"I don't think we should discuss this here, we need to get back to the village," Sari stepped in. "Can you walk?" She asked Tori, who only nodded numbly. "I promise, I will answer all your questions once we are back in the village." Allen seemed satisfied for now.

"We have to go with them T-bird. We need to find

Dean, right?" Allen asked softly. He looked up the hill they were about to climb and Tori watched as his gaze fell on Sari and lingered. He shook his head, ever so slightly then turned his attention back to Tori, "Let me help you." He wrapped his arm around her waist and together they started through the woods and up the incline of the sloping terrain.

"Allen?" Tori whispered, "I'm scared."

"Me too."

CHAPTER FOUR

The Village

The village was set deep in the forest, a forest which was unlike anything Tori had ever seen. There was no path, so the going was slow especially with Tori's injured ankle. As they made their way through the shady twists and turns of the forest, Tori began to really see how different their surroundings were from home. The tree trunks, around which they dodged and turned, led twenty or so feet to gangly arms which bore fruit.

Tori's grandparents had once owned an apple farm, which used to visit every summer. She spent countless hours climbing the limbs of those trees with her grandfather trimming trees nearby. The branches made for easy climbing but the trees never grew more than 8-10 feet high. These were enormous fruit trees of all varieties. Intertwined between the fruit trees were dark green stalks that reached above the tallest branches of the trees, opening to gigantic yellow-brown plumes.

"Are those sunflowers?!" Tori said in disbelief.

"Little bigger than the ones back home, huh?" Allen said lightly.

The underbrush was not scrub oak and chokecherries but dwarf pines and birch trees. Tiny strips of bark peeled away from tiny paper birch trunks and acorns the size of a grape seed hung from miniature oak trees.

They started up another gradual incline which took all of Tori's strength to conquer. Her ankle throbbed but she wasn't leaning on Allen anymore. She limped heavily, but her fear helped push the pain to the back of her mind. She gripped the stalks of the sunflowers and the fruit trees for leverage as she climbed the muddy slope. The air was growing thick and muggy, like it may rain, but soon the smell of a campfire wafted over the crest of the hill telling them they were close.

Tori tripped as she crested the top of the hill and landed on her hands and knees, breathing heavy with exertion. When she stood again, she found they were at the head of a trail. Down the trail she could see a small plume of smoke rising up to the sky.

"The village is just down here," Sari said, helping Allen over the edge of the hill. The forest floor was clearer here, with much less underbrush and foliage to wade through. The trail led them to a large clearing amongst the trees revealing, finally, the village.

The village of Everidge was built into the landscape with homes made into the large boulders at the edge of the clearing. High in the boughs of the fruit trees, tree houses hung connected to one another by wooden bridges and ropes. At the base of the sunflower stalks, smaller domiciles were nestled. The sunlight was burning low in the sky but the village felt warm and almost cozy to Tori.

As they entered the clearing a small animal ran to meet them. It was the size of a pig and a strange shade of grey. Its face was flat with two floppy ears on each side of its head and a long snout in the center.

"Is that a…."

"An elephant? Yes." Sari said, finishing Allen's sentence as she scooped up the creature in her arms endearingly. "This is Eloise." Sari could see the shock coming off Allen and Tori in waves. "There's going to be a lot of new things in the next few days, I will do my best to explain what I can after we get you settled, yeah?"

"Settled? Wait, you mean stay here?!" Tori felt her heart begin to race and choke her breathing. Her breaths came fast and she tried to grasp onto something, anything to calm herself down before the panic took her completely. "How do we get home?!" Tori could hear her voice rising but couldn't control it. Sari set Eloise down and came to Tori.

"Tori," she said softly, "you need to calm down."

"Calm down?! Calm DOWN! I can't calm down! I have no idea where I am, what is going on and you want me to calm DOWN!" Sari stepped nose to nose with her, stopping her mid-rant.

"If you want to survive, you cannot panic. If you panic, you jeopardize everyone in this village. Do you understand?" Tori nodded, confused and scared.

Hadn't she spent the last year of her life being scared?

Sari sighed, she looked tired.

From across the village came a blood curdling scream, making all four of them flinch.

"NO GET AWAY FROM ME! GET AWAY FROM ME!"

Forgetting the pain in her ankle she was sprinting across the village towards Dean's voice before she could even think.

CHAPTER FIVE

Dreams

Dean was in a strange bed in small, one-room house. The smell of a fireplace tickled his nostrils. Raw logs and stone used to construct the walls were visible from the inside of the room. Pitchers and baskets hung from pegs in the crossbeams of the ceiling. A simple basin sink was across the room from where he lay in bed. A ladder ascended to a second story on the left and the wooden front door was to his right. Dean lifted himself up on one elbow and pain flared across his chest. He fell back onto to the bed, pain thrumming through his rib cage. He must have broken a rib.

A dark fog suddenly settled over the cottage, the smell of sulfur and coal filled the air. His breath quickened against his rib's protests. The iron door knob slowly began to turn, and the door pushed open as a huge dark figure ducked in through the doorway. A swell of red and black clouds followed him into the small room. The heavy sound of iron clad footfalls echoed against the rock, Dean stared up in horror at the enormous creature towering above him. He wasn't quite a man, but not all monster either. Dressed solely in black, the man spoke in a deep, rumbling tone that reverberated deep in Dean's bones.

"There you are…. Pretty Boy!" With snakelike speed, he reached behind his head and unsheathed a sword and brought the gigantic blade down in the middle of Dean's chest.

Dean began to scream...

"Dean, it's me! I'm here," Tori was leaning over him, hands on his cheeks. Dean threw his head to the side frantically scanning the room for the man in black, but the smoke had cleared and the sulfur smell no longer hung in the air, infiltrating his senses. He exhaled in relief and let his head drop back against the bed.

"Tori, I had a horrible dream, there was smoke and…" He heard a gurgle from Tori. Dean opened his eyes and lifted his head. "Tori?" Tori was staring at him but did not see him, her mouth moved in a strangled, gulping motion. Dean struggled to sit up and grab Tori by the shoulders, "What is it? Tori, what happened?" Tori's body convulsed, Dean looked down and saw the blade from the man in black's glint in the light. It ripped through the front of Tori's body just below the sternum, her crimson blood spread out across her shirt and dripping down the front of the blade. "No…" Dean put his hand to the wound but could not stop the blood. "No!" He looked at her beautiful face, which was now streaked with blood, her amber eyes swimming in a sea of red. The whites of her eyes had been completely drowned out by dark pools of blood.

Tori gurgled again then whispered, "He's coming for you, Pretty Boy!"

Screams filled Dean's ears as hands clamped down on his appendages, struggling to hold him down.

"NO GET AWAY! GOD NO!"

Tori, Allen, the twins and 2 women that Tori didn't know struggled to keep Dean down so he didn't further injure himself.

"What's happening to him?" Tori screamed over the chaos.

"They're in his head..... They're coming for him," The older woman answered as she ground furiously on some concoction in a mortar and pestle. "Open his mouth," Seth laid an arm over Dean's chest, holding him firm to the mattress as Sari tilted back his head and opened his mouth. Dean arched his back and raged against the restraint. Tori let go of the arm she was holding and stepped back, hands to her mouth, in horror. A small, short haired girl grabbed the flailing arm Tori had dropped and held fast. Her hair was a red flash as she swooped in.

What is happening? Tori thought in a panic.

The older woman poured the mixture into Dean's mouth, Sari clamped his mouth closed again and held her hand over it until he swallowed. After several minutes Dean finally relaxed his body back onto the bed. His eyes opened and, though drowsy from whatever they had just given him, he was awake and calm.

"He should be able to rest now." The older woman sighed. The rest slowly released their grips on him and stepped away in exhaustion. Dean was calm now but he desperately scanned the faces of each person in the room, exhaling in relief when he found Tori.

"Are you real?" His voice was raw from screaming. Tori choked out the tears that had been caught in her throat.

"Yes, I'm real."

CHAPTER SIX

Allen

Allen closed the door behind him as he followed Sari out of the cottage, leaving Tori alone with Dean who was resting peacefully now. The older woman, named Millie, had left as well to restock her herbs.

Allen leaned back against the stone cottage and doubled over, his head reeling. He tried to calm himself, taking deep breaths but his mind spun with everything it was asked to take in.

"Allen?" Sari put her hand on his back but her voice sounded far away. "Just breathe." Slowly the world stopped tilting on its axis and he stood.

"What the hell was that Sari?" Allen was terrified by what he had just seen. Sari was quiet for a moment.

"Let's take a walk, yeah?"

"Okay,"

They walked casually back through the village, weaving underneath a network of treehouses and bridges. Eloise scampered over from a shaded area under a huge lily. Sari stopped and bent over and picked up the elephant.

"We have a few of these little buggers roaming around the village, but she's my favorite," Allen didn't reply. He watched how gentle Sari was, and how her white gold hair fell over her shoulders and how her brilliant eyes shimmers every time they passed from the shade to streams of sunlight. She was surreally beautiful.

"The Caligo are... different" Sari started off, to which Allen laughed.

"You're going to have to put 'different' in context for me," he gestured to the stalk of giant sunflower as he said this.

"Touché. All the humans here came the same way you did, through the Portis. Others were born here, they're the natives."

"The Caligo,"

"No one knows exactly how long the Portis has been there but we are fairly sure that the Caligo created it. They prey upon humans. They use them as slaves in the mines."

Sari leaned down and let Eloise scoot out of her arms and trot away. She motioned for Allen to come with her down a small trail that wound into the woods. The afternoon light filtered through the trees in hazy streams giving the wood an ethereal quality. The moss that covered the trees was brilliant green against the dark bark of the fruit trees. The small evergreens covered the ground between the trees like ferns, blanketing the forest floor in a sea of green.

"Because the Caligo are of this world they are not bound by restrictions of another world like we are." Allen sensed something really bad was coming. "The Caligo can enter our dreams. They can manipulate them and basically slowly drive the dreamer insane. Eventually, the Caligo don't need to waste the time to come here and kidnap us. Their victims, whoever they choose, go to them."

"They bring us to them, like cattle." Allen walked quietly for a moment. He was not remotely prepared to deal with this! "So they want Dean then?" he finally asked.

"It seems so. He's a good friend of yours?" Sari asked. Allen actually laughed.

"No, I mean he's all right, but I just met the guy. He and Tori are..."

"Oh I thought maybe you and she were," Sari stammered. Was she nervous? Allen never had this effect on girls like Sari.

"Me and T? No." He was honestly shocked that she even cared. "We grew up together; she's really my only family." Sari looked up at him with sympathy in her eyes. "My dad wasn't around, having kids didn't suit him. And my mom died not long ago."

Why was he telling her this? They walked in silence for a moment letting the trail wind them through the woods down to a river. A small foot path led to the river's edge where a boulder sat perfectly like a bench. Sari nodded toward it and they turned their course and sat in the sunlight.

"I come here a lot." She said softly, watching the water flow past in frothy ripples. Allen's arm brushed hers and he stiffened immediately and his stomach clenched. He hadn't felt this awkward since middle school.

"So," he cleared his throat and tried to recover some swagger, "You and Seth came through the Portis together then?"

Sari nodded, "We met at my farm, where I kept a small plot with sheep, for our birthday. We went out back and that's when we saw them."

"The meteors."

"The meteors. Then there was this blinding light and this horrible sound, it knocked us right to the ground. Once we got ourselves upright again, there it was… Right in the back yard. I can't describe it, it's like it called me."

"Me too," Allen said solemnly.

"Then it seemed to grab me, and drag me."

"Then you were stuck."

"Exactly!" Sari turned to him, relieved someone else had had the same experience.

"I'm afraid of the answer but, how long have you been here?" Sari's smiled faded at Allen's question; she rubbed her eyes, tiredly.

"Allen, I will tell you everything, I will, but I think the rest needs to be saved for all three of you. It's... a lot."

Allen laughed again; he was feeling a little crazier every second.

"Seriously, how much worse can it get?" When Sari only stared at him, he stopped laughing. "Oh god, how much worse can it get?"

Sari sighed again, and turned towards Allen. Their knees touched, momentarily distracting Allen.

"When Seth and I came through the Portis..." Sari spoke calmly and evenly but her gaze never wavered, she held Allen's eyes, "we were 60 years old." Allen's initial reaction was laughter but when he saw how she neither flinched nor so much as cracked a smile, his whole body filled with dread.

"But wait, you're my age. How can that be unless...." The words caught in his throat.

"I've been here 40 years, Allen. I'm 102." Sari turned back toward the river letting what she had said settle.

"So once you're here, you get..."

"Younger." Sari confirmed. Allen's head spun

again and he put his head down in his hands. This couldn't really be happening, could it? Sari reached over and took his hand sympathetically. "See why I wanted to wait?" Allen choked out a laugh and nodded.

"So do you always get the awesome job of telling the newbies this?"

"We take turns being the bearer of bad news, Millie more than others." Allen sat up regaining his composure, or at least pretending to. He could freak out later.

"Why is that?"

"She's been here the longest," Sari shrugged, but Allen was confused

"But how's that possible? She's old… um older." Allen was suddenly very aware he was talking to an old lady in a beautiful girl's skin.

"All we really know is that at some point she was a prisoner of the Caligo, I'm not sure how long they had her but when she finally escaped she was different. She hasn't aged – either way- since,"

"Did they do to her what they are trying to do to Dean?"

"No, she was out at our farms and they just took her. That's all I really know. She won't talk about it."

"If they can take us by force, why drive us crazy in our sleep?" This perplexed Allen.

"Well first of all, the sunflower trees are toxic to them. Second of all, why risk a battle when you can make your prey come to you?" Allen nodded, it made sense. They were basically sitting ducks against the Caligo and he and his friends were fresh meat. The thought was unsettling. He turned back to Sari who was looking out onto the river again, her hair blowing in the breeze.

"102, huh?"

"102." Sari confirmed without looking at him, trying to hide her shame or embarrassment, Allen couldn't tell which. Allen was quiet for a minute.

"You know, I dig older chicks." Allen nudged her with his arm, Sari turned to him shocked but smiling. Sari laughed and shoved him back. "So where are the farms?" Allen asked changing the subject.

"Come see," she grabbed his arm, dragging him off the rock further down the trail which branched off to the right and opened to a large field. On the right side of the field sat a small stone structure. Then Allen saw them. He was amazed.

CHAPTER SEVEN

Tori

Tori sat on the floor of the cottage, knees to her chest and head laid back against the side of Dean's pillow. Everyone had left once he had settled down, leaving her alone with him, which scared her a little. What would she do if, whatever that was, happened again? She sighed heavily. Dean rolled his head to the side behind her, his breath caressing her neck, awakening goosebumps down her neck and arms. She smiled because despite everything, she was with Dean and Allen who would protect her. Thinking about anything else, made her head hurt. She knew that she shouldn't be so relieved to be so weak, but she had no idea on how to change it either.

"Tori?" Dean mumbled making Tori jump. She turned and smiled at him as she leaned her elbow against his pillow.

"Hey," she whispered when his eyes finally focused on her, he smiled.

"Hey back," He looked around the cottage confused, "Where are we? What happened?" Millie had said his memory might be fuzzy.

"Do you want the long or the short version?"

"Short please," his voice was weary still from the herbs he'd been given.

"Well, we came through some kind of doorway called a Portis and we ended up here. Everidge? It's some kind of medieval village place." Tori perked suddenly, "But they have HUGE sunflowers here Dean! They are like trees!" Dean laughed at her enthusiasm but the motion sent him doubled over in pain. "Oh, and you have a broken rib or two." Tori laid her chin on her forearm and looked closely at Dean, "How do you feel?" Dean reached up and stroked her cheek with his thumb.

"I'm better now."

Tori's cheeks flushed and her stomach danced with butterflies. Things felt almost normal for a moment.

"You scared me you know," Tori whispered, "What were you dreaming about?" Dean lay back on the bed and shook his head.

"There was this guy, all in black armor and he... he..." Dean closed his eyes against the memory but he continued, "he kept coming for me, and" Dean opened his eyes again as he realized something. "He kept calling me Pretty Boy." Tori's blood turned cold.

"Just like Beau...."

CHAPTER EIGHT

Allen

The herd of cows was unlike anything Allen had ever seen. Just as Eloise was miniaturized, the cows were gigantic. They stood nearly fifteen feet tall; their legs were as thick around as a small tree trunk. They shuffled around and grazed in the huge field, every once in a while one would bellow out a "moo," making Allen jump. Sari snickered.

"This is where we get most of our food, we have a small garden off of the barn but one of these cows will feed the entire village for a month," Sari explained.

"Yeah! I bet!" Allen gasped, "They're HUGE! And the Caligo don't steal them?" noticing the field butted up to the bottom of the mountain where the tribe lived.

"They don't eat what we eat," she said cryptically. "They're cannibals."

It just kept getting better. How were these people surviving living in the shadow of the Caligo? Allyn guessed only because the Caligo were allowing them to.

"We should get back, it will be dusk soon and the insects will soon be out."

"Lemme guess, the bugs are huge, too," Allen joked, but when Sari only smiled apologetically at him, he whined. "Ah man."

CHAPTER NINE

The residents of the Vale all gathered at sunset and raised a giant thatch dome over the village. The protective dome was pulled up by ropes connected to pulleys hanging high in the trees; the dome closed roughly over the village above the tree line and was secured at the base of a central tree holding it in place. Tori didn't like not being able to see the sky clearly, it gave her a feeling of claustrophobia, but once she saw what came out of the night, she was glad it was there. Sari and Allen made it back into the village just as the dome was coming up from a small trail that led into the woods. Sari quickly helped secured the ropes; Seth soon joined her handing her a bow and quiver of arrows. Sari smiled back at Allen then left the village center with her brother.

"Hey, how's Dean?" Allen asked Tori as he walked up to her.

"He's okay…. But we need to talk. Alone." Tori whispered pulling Allen around the side of Millie's house.

"What's going on T-bird?" Allen asked concerned creasing his face. Tori didn't even know where to start.

"Dean's dreams…. Beau is in his dreams, Allen. Attacking him in his dreams."

"How is that even possible?" Allen asked, piling more confusion into brain.

"Millie told us that if he is using the dreams to attack Dean *here*, in this world, he must be here. They said the Portis isn't stable, it can remain open for any length of time….. He could've followed us here," Tori felt the anxiety twist in her stomach, threatening to block her intake of oxygen.

"As bad as that is, it's about to get a lot worse." Allen sighed.

"How can this get WORSE?!" Tori shrieked.

"Shhh!" Allen hissed. "Just listen."

CHAPTER TEN

Tori

Tori was numb. Her head spun as she reentered Millie's cottage with Allen close behind. The cracks and hisses of the creatures crawling up the side of the dome were starting to drive Tori crazy so she had rushed back into the safety of the cottage. Dean was sitting up now, propped up by pillows and blankets, seeming to be in slightly less pain. He held a clay bowl in his hands as Millie fussed over him and hovered nearby. Dean's face brightened when he saw Tori walk in but concern soon clouded his expression when he saw the distress on Tori's face.

"What's wrong love? You look as if you've seen a ghost." Millie spoke with a heavy Scottish accent that made her that much more lovable. She was so outwardly maternal that Tori resisted the urge to crumple into her arms crying. As if reading her thoughts Millie put an arm around her shoulders and Tori let her head fall into Millie's embrace.

"It's so much to take in isn't it?"

Tori nodded miserably.

"What's going on?" Dean asked from across the room.

"We have some things to talk about," Allen said shutting the door.

CHAPTER ELEVEN

Sari

"It certainly complicates things if a Caligo is hunting specifically for you, doesn't it?" Sari said thoughtfully. Filling her in on Dean's dreams and Millie's theory on Beau had been far easier than explaining to Dean the age reversal. He was still quiet. Absorbing it all.

"If he were with the Caligo, wouldn't they just make him a slave?" Tori said from the bed next to Dean.

"Or dinner?" Everyone looked over at Allen horrified. "Seriously, it couldn't happen to a nicer guy." Allen smiled.

"Typically yes, anyone they capture from the Portis usually begins working in the mines immediately. Well until…"

"We get it." Tori snapped, cutting off Sari and holding up her hands in exasperation. Sari felt for the girl. She seems perpetually nervous and this place was not for the faint of heart.

"Not always," Millie said quietly from the kitchen area of the room where she mixed something in a bowl. "I've seen them take newcomers into their army."

Everyone stared at her. Sari had never heard of this and was shocked Millie had kept this from her.

"Why would they recruit humans?" Tori asked.

"Humans can be just as monstrous as the Caligo. After some... alteration, they can be just as formidable."

"Alterations?" Sari asked.

"They have an alchemist and they mix potions same as I do, theirs are much more potent. Can do horrifying things. Like turn a man into a monster just like Lucius."

"You've never said anything about this," Sari was angry that such things had been kept when people's lives hung in the balance. She tried to steady herself and calm herself down.

"Wait a sec. Who's Lucius?" Dean asked.

"Their leader. He's evil. He, and few of his men, were chasing us this morning."

Everyone was silent for a moment as it settled in how truly unpleasant a situation they were in. Tori and Dean sat close on the bed, but her face was filled with terror and her hands shook terribly. She was trying her best to hide her fear but Sari felt it coming off of her like a wave. Allen and Sari were seated in chairs near the fireplace while Millie continued to busy herself about the kitchen as she always did. Seth was out doing rounds at the barrier, which is what Sari should be doing, but Allen and his friends needed her here. Tori suddenly jumped up from the bed, startling everyone.

"I need some air," she mumbled as she quickly exited the cabin.

"Allen maybe you should go with her," Dean suggested.

"Let the girl be…. The poor lass needs some time," Millie chided from the kitchen. No one argued and the room fell into a comfortable silence.

CHAPTER TWELVE

Tori

Tori had to get out of that room. She was suffocating. The air outside felt cool and heavenly against her skin. She put her head back, letting the breeze lick her cheek and calm her racing heart rate.

As she settled a noise from above her head caught her attention. She turned and from between the braided pieced of vine and branches making up the dome stuck an antennae as big as she was. It flicked around, tasting the air for food. Tori stepped around the edge of the cottage, eyes wide to get a better look.

The head of the massive centipede was above her but the body trailed down the dome to the ground. It seemed too big to be real. The centipede's antennae suddenly sensed her presence and began twitching earnestly in her direction, awakening the entire insect with hunger. It writhed its giant body against the dome, desperate to get to her.

Tori started stepping away carefully, suppressing the scream in her throat, when she bumped into something letting the scream escape. A hand immediately clasped over her mouth. She almost began a whole new fit of hysteria when she saw Seth's face in the moonlight. He motioned with a finger to his lips for her to be quiet.

"Screaming will just make it more agitated." He took his hand away from her mouth slowly, making sure she was done screaming. "C'mon,"

He turned suddenly and walked away, leaving Tori standing there, stunned, with the monster centipede behind her. She looked around in confusion then ran to catch up. She silently fell into step with him.

"The bugs take getting used to," he said, after they had crossed the village clearing. "Spiders are the worst." Tori looked over at him in horror. "There are scorpions closer to the mountain that are as big as cars," he laughed ever so slightly. "Even the butterflies are bloody terrifying,"

They wove easily between the trees and then they slipped between two cottages near the edge of the dome on the valley side of the village.

"But these… are my favorite" Seth pulled back a low hanging cherry limb to reveal a small clearing in the woods. Tori looked through the openings in the thatch dome as the valley lit in a dance of green lights. The fireflies were as big as hot air balloons and when they shone their lights they lit Tori and Seth's faces. Tori didn't speak, or breathe. She had never seen anything so beautiful. The lights appeared and disappeared in this beautiful rhythm that rendered Tori speechless. They hovered not far from the ground so the valley looked like an iridescent green pool. It looked like magic.

"It's beautiful," Tori breathed.

"It is…" Seth agreed. Tori looked over at him and saw him staring her, not the fireflies. She scoffed a bit and smiled.

"I meant the fireflies," she laughed looking back to the valley.

"I know. I meant you, love." Seth smiled as Tori again looked over at him in surprise. Even with the green iridescence lighting up his face, his eyes were still shining a stunning blue.

Is this happening? Did I faint back there?

"I should get ba…." As Tori began to stammer out her exit, a spider dropped down the outside of the dome. Suspended by its web, it hissed and spit, clicking its legs against the branches of the dome. With one swift movement, Seth pulled his spear from under his cloak and stabbed the mammoth spider through the thorax. It shrieked, as did Tori, then fell to the ground as Seth retracted his spear. Seth sighed.

"Tomorrow," he said.

Tori shook her head in confusion. "What?"

"Tomorrow I teach you how to defend yourself," he wiped his spear on his pant leg, then turned and started back across the village. "Let's get you back." Tori stared after him for a minute.

"Why?" she called.

Seth stopped and turned back towards her. "Why what?"

"Why are you going to teach me? I mean, I appreciate it, but I didn't ask."

"Because you look like someone who is sick of getting rescued. And you didn't need to ask." Seth smiled.

It occurred to Tori at that moment that she WAS sick of being rescued. And had been for a long time.

Seth returned Tori safely back to Millie's. As he opened the door for her, he bent in close and whispered, "Goodnight beautiful," in her ear. Tori's whole body trembled and electricity ignited on her neck where his breath had touch her skin.

Sari saw the look on Tori's face and furrowed her brow at her brother.

"What's going on Seth?" Sari asked him curtly. Seth smiled very devilishly at his sister and closed the door between them, returning to his rounds. Tori's cheeks burned. She quickly sat down awkwardly next to Dean, who took her hand.

"You okay?" he asked her, sweetly.

"Yeah, Seth's going to teach me how to defend myself," she said proudly.

"Good… just be careful," Dean said softly. Tori prickled at his response.

"Here you go love," Millie said, handing Dean a bitter smelling concoction. "It will help with the dreams and let you rest" As she handed Dean the cup Tori noticed the shiny scarring on her hands. The scar tissue stretched against her knuckles as she moved her hand. Whatever had happened to her had been painful; the scars were deep and angry. When Millie caught her staring, she quickly covered her hands in embarrassment and went back into the kitchen. Tori opened her mouth to say something, anything that would take away the embarrassment she had caused this kind woman. But there were no words. Just a sour pit of shame in Tori's stomach.

CHAPTER THIRTEEN

Allen

Allen had lucked out last night. When it came time to get him and Tori settled into their own cottages, he got a tree house. He had felt like a kid. But this morning the allure had worn off. The morning light felt wrong. It wasn't the soft light that eases in a day, \; it was much harsher, like that of midafternoon. The burnt color of the sky spoke of sunset, not the clear soft colors of sunrise. It made Allen uneasy. His distaste for the lighting soon dissipated when he heard a knock at the door. Allen yelled for Sari to come in, quickly flattening his bedhead with his hands.

Sunlight streamed in the door after her, igniting her hair into white flames. Her blue eyes, as brilliant as always, made him weak kneed. She wasn't wearing the cloak this morning, so he could see her slender frame through her thin clothing. She smiled at him.

"I am heading out, care to join me? I want to introduce you to some people."

How could he refuse? "Sure," he smiled.

The sunlight was no less harsh outside but as sunrise waned into late morning, the sky lighted to a cool blue. The dome had come down some time after the sun had come up when the giant bugs had all retreated. Seth and another man were busy tacking it the ground;

they paused when they saw Sari and Allen approaching.

"Allen, this is Roth." Roth stood to meet Allen who was not only dwarfed by Roth but completely intimidated by him. Roth was as solid mass of muscle. Even next to Seth, who was tall and brawny, Roth looked enormous. His dark skin and eyes were a stark contrast to Seth's pale complexion and hair as well. Roth offered Allen his hand.

"Good to meet you, welcome to Everidge." Roth said, taking Allen's hand. Allen thought his hand might break in Roth's grip, but Roth's obvious good nature put Allen at ease.

"Roth's been with us six years and he is invaluable to us," Sari smiled warmly at him and Roth was genuinely humbled by her praise.

"Nice to meet you Roth," Allen said.

"And Seth, you've already met. Seth who will be behaving himself today, yeah?" she loudly barked at him.

"Yeah, yeah." Seth winked at her and went back to work, "Hurry up Roth, I've got a date!"

"Seth!" Sari hissed. Roth and Seth laughed as they went back to work.

"Sometimes it really bloody sucks being stuck for eternity with your brother," she shook her head as she led Allen across Everidge.

"Hey, I was thinking about that. You said the Portis opens from time to time, people *have* gone back right? Back home?" Allen asked as Eloise bounded out of the bushes to meet them.

"Yes."

"Then why didn't you and Seth ever go home?"

She didn't answer for a moment. She finally shrugged, "No reason to go home, if there is no one there waiting for you." She smiled, but her eyes were sad. "No one we even knew would even be alive now anyway. We were needed here." She continued walking but Allen stopped short. She had chosen an eternity of this because these people had needed help. Allen's mind wrapped around the idea of Sari then, around who she was and who she had been. Everything he needed to know about her, he knew.

"You coming?" And that accent was great too, Allen thought as Sari smiled at him.

They came upon one of the larger cottages situated between two taller fruit trees. A large overhang shaded the front of the building. Much like the interior of Millie's house, pitchers and baskets hung from the beams of the pavilion. In the shade sat two girls. One with long black tendrils and a pointy nose sat with a stone platter in front of her chopping a vegetable that was completely unknown to Allen. The other girl Allen recognized from the afternoon before, he remembered her short, red pixie cut even amongst the chaos of Dean's dream assault. She had been there helping keep him still, and then had disappeared before anyone could talk to her. Now she sat with a wooden bowl balanced on her knees, kneading dough with her hands.

"This is Madalyn and Paige," Sari said. Allen smiled politely and said hello. They moved along quickly.

"Paige was at Millie's yesterday wasn't she?" Allen asked once out of earshot.

"Yes, she helps out a lot."

"Why didn't she say anything?"

"She's had a hard time since getting here. The dreams happened to her as well shortly after she arrived. Millie couldn't control them so Paige tried." Sari's tone grew very dark and hushed

"What did she do?"

"She slit her wrists."

Allen stopped in his tracks at Sari's words. Sari stopped and took his hand, "She's okay now, and we keep an eye on her. Dean will be okay, too."

Sari and Allen headed back down to the fields and made their way to the barn. Moving amongst the enormous cattle was daunting to say the least. Allen froze in fear as one wandered over towards him, when it only nosed him and shook its head Allen relaxed. They ducked into the barn and were greeted by a small tough looking woman dragging a bridle down the hallway.

"Hey, Annie? Where's Dru?" Sari asked, cheerfully.

"Back here!" A square jawed man stepped out from a back room.

"Allen, this is Dru and Annie. They tend the livestock," Sari smiled. "And they are fantastic at it!"

"Keep sweet talking Sari," Dru said as he smiled. "Nice to meet you Allen," Annie nodded.

"Dru was a horse guy or some sort back home," Sari began.

"I trained champions!" Dru interjected.

"Well now he is determined to tame one of the wolves you saw yesterday," Sari stepped deeper into the barn to a back stall. A huge, furry mass slept in the corner of the stall. It was smaller than the ones he had seen the previous day. But it was definitely one of the Caligo's wolves.

"I will be riding him by summer!" Dru called from the front of the barn.

Sari laughed. "Let's go."

They wandered up the trail in silence, Allen taking in the strange beauty of this world. Lilies, his mother's favorite flower, grew in giant bunches like palm trees. They entered the woods again and passed the river trail Sari had taken him down the day before. Allen stopped at the junction of the trails, deep in thought.

"If everyone gets younger," Allen almost didn't want to ask the question for fear of the answer, "Everyone, besides Millie, is my age. Shouldn't there be kids here?"

Sari nodded. "I'm not sure you want to meet them. It isn't," she struggled for the words, "what you think."

"I need to wrap my mind around all of this Sari, please take me." Allen took her hand. After hesitating, Sari nodded.

They ascended a ladder leading up the trunk of a cherry tree near Millie's house, where Allen figured Tori still sat vigilant over Dean. The cottage was masked in shadows of branches and leaves. Sari pushed open the door, stepping into the deep shadows of the room. Allen followed her in and let his eyes adjust to the darkness. Several beds lined the walls, only a few cradled small bodies. They approached a bed at the far side of the room, a bony frame poked out from beneath the thin blankets as he rolled towards them.

"This is Jacob… he was 16 when he came through, he's been here five years…." Sari reached down and softly pushed Jacob's hair from his hot forehead. "Once our bodies get to about nine years of age physically, they degrade and…."

"Die," Jacob whispered. Sari retrieved a cool cloth from a nearby basin and put it on his head. Jacob's large eyes were black discs sunken into his skull; grey circles swirled at the skin around his lashes. Then Allen suddenly realized what everyone in Everidge had in common. Their eyes. Everyone's eyes were haunted by the grey shadows. Even Sari's blazing blue eyes were rimmed with the grey swirls.

"Rest Jacob," Sari nodded towards the door, Allen followed gratefully.

In the daylight again, Allen took a long deep breath of the fresh air. He leaned against the railing letting his thoughts settle.

"We're all going to end up like that aren't we?"

"No," Sari said sternly grabbing Allen but the shoulders and standing him up, face to face with her, "We will get you home."

"Why not send them through the Portis?"

"We're not sure they would survive the journey."

"His eyes… Everyone here has those grey eyes." He took Sari's hands in his. "How long do you and Seth really have?"

"We don't know. We think a few more years but because we have been here so long, we could be on borrowed time. But we'd be dead if we weren't here, if we were home. So I figure, every day we get, is one more day we were given for a reason. She looked down at their intertwined hands and smiled. "I was sick when I got here, Allen. Stage 4 lung cancer. I was on my third round of Chemo but, it wasn't working. Once a got here, over time, I got healthier. I *felt* healthier." She struck a seductive pose, "I mean look at me!" she laughed.

"You do look pretty fabulous to me," Allen smiled at her. Then a thought occurred to him. "What about Millie?"

"What about her?" Sari asked confused.

"You said that the Caligo did something to her to stop the aging process. Can't we find out what they did and recreate it?"

"She won't talk about it, Allen." Sari started toward the ladder.

"Sari, everyone here is our age physically. Pretty soon this village will be empty!"

"I will try and talk to her. But right now we have something more important to tend to."

"What's that?"

"We have to teach you how to fight."

CHAPTER FOURTEEN

Tori

Tori needed to get some fresh air. She felt like she had been in this tiny cottage forever. Millie walked outside with her, wringing her hands in her apron.

"Another day or so and he will be up and around."

"Okay, I can hang in there until he is ready," Tori sighed.

"You don't need to do that honey," Millie said kindly, "Go out and explore." Tori hesitated and Millie took her by the arm. "Love, he's not going to miss you and you will be fine on your own."

Millie directed her into the village clearing and pointed over her shoulder "Don't go past the river and stay in the forest, if you get to the valley you've gone too far." She squeezed Tori's arm, "You need to learn to exist on your own little one." Tori nodded, knowing she was right.

Tori gingerly stepped away from the cottage and headed across the village. Eloise trotted out to meet her. She stopped and patted the strange little creature who danced with happiness. Tori toured the village and soon, with no panic biting at her, she stood at the top of a small hill looking down into a gully lined with the strange, giant flowers and fruit trees. Across the gully Seth was busy hanging a thatch target to the trunk of one of the flower trees. When he turned to retrieve his bow and quiver, he noticed her standing at the top of the rise. She felt heat rise to her face.

"Sorry, I didn't know you were down here. I can go." Tori turned to go.

"No!" Seth yelled, then looking a little embarrassed himself, he tried again. "No, come down. I said I would teach you." He held up his bow and smiled, his confidence obviously regained. Tori couldn't resist. She felt a pang of guilt at the thought of Dean lying broken and beaten in Millie's. If it wasn't for her, he wouldn't even *be* here.

She was so sick of feeling guilty. And anxious. And afraid.

"Sure. Show me." She slid down the hill taking Seth's hand to steady herself. She let go quickly and followed Seth to a mark in the earth. Seth took Tori by the waist, and lined her up with the target. Tori held her breath at his touch.

"Ever shot one of these before?"

"I think once at summer camp... like eight years ago!" she laughed.

"Okay you've got your bow here... Are you right or left handed?" Seth asked.

"Right,"

"Okay, take the bow in your left hand and the bow string in your right hand." He held his hand over hers on the wooden bow then reached around her back and put is other hand over her right hand on the bow string. She felt the heat of his body against her back, her skin tingled and goosebumps rose on her arms.

Get ahold of yourself Tori! Focus!

"Pull the string back with your right hand until the string is taut and can't go any further." She felt his muscle tense against hers as they pulled the string back. "You want to hold the string with just 2 fingers." He gently put pressure on her index and middle finger, pressing them around the string. Then he moved his hand and softly took her ring and pinkie finger off the string, trailing his hand down her wrist. He leaned in close and Tori felt the whisper of his lips against her neck causing her to involuntarily release the bowstring suddenly. Seth jumped back.

Jesus, Tori!

"Whoa! Warn me before you do that again, yeah?"

"I could say the same to you," Tori countered. Seth smiled and shrugged innocently.

"Let's try again, yeah?" He set her up again then stepped back and grabbed an arrow from the quiver and set it carefully into her grip. "The left index finger is going to be the cradle for the front of the arrow, the back two hold the arrow to the string." He seated the arrow for her and stepped back. "Try and focus on the target and line the tip of the arrow up and…"

Tori released the string, sending the arrow just left of the target.

"Crap…" she mumbled.

"That actually wasn't bad!" Seth sounded impressed. "But you rushed it. This time, before you release it, take a breath. Slow down. It's better to have a slow shot that hits its mark than a fast shot that misses." He took another arrow from the quiver and handed it to her. This time Tori seated the arrow herself and pulled it back with only minimal difficulty. Keeping the arrow in place while you pulled the string back was a little tricky, but she did it. She lined the arrowhead up with the target then took a slow breath in. And released the string.

Thunk!

"You hit it!" Seth cheered.

"I did? Oh my god, I did!" Tori looked at the arrow sticking into the target just inside the left side of the target in disbelief.

"Okay, now this time," Seth was already handing her another arrow, "aim a little more right. You drift a little left."

Tori took the arrow from him, smiling excitedly. As the adrenaline pump through her veins, she carefully set the arrow and stretched back the string. She focused as she had done before, and then adjusted slightly to her right.

Deep breath.

She released the arrow.

Thunk!

"Bulls eye!" Seth yelled throwing his arms above his head in celebration. Tori whooped in triumph and jumped excitedly in the air.

"Did you see that?! That was awesome!" She screamed. She jumped again right into Seth's arms. She wrapped her arms around her neck and he spun her. Once they both stopped spinning, Tori got ahold of herself and quickly slid out of his arms and backed away a step. She looked down a little embarrassed, pushing a stray piece of hair behind her ear. "Thank you Seth. I needed this." Tori handed him back the bow a little reluctantly and turned to go.

"Lesson's not over." Seth took her arm. "We still have spears, knives…. Lots more to cover." Seth smiled devilishly at her, but his eyes also asked her not to go.

"Well, then I can't disappoint the professor," she teased.

Seth slowly took a step toward her, bring his hand to her cheek he traced his thumb along her jawline. His touch was electric. Sending a tingling sensation tricking across her skin at his and heat pulsating through her body.

"Where have you been?" Seth whispered, coming in closer. "It feels like I've been waiting for you forever."

The world around them stopped and went silent. In that moment it was just the two of them. Tori brought her hand her cheek and intertwined her fingers with his. She leaned into his touch.   Seth's intense blue eyes burned into her, filtered through the mess of her neurotic personality and saw *her*. Who she was and who she could be. Who she wanted to be.

"Hey!" a voice yelled from the up the hill. Tori jumped back, the spell broken. She looked up the rise to see the girl with red pixie cut hair, from the day before. She looked from Tori to Seth and back again with an accusatory glare. "Am I interrupting something?"

"What do need Paige?" Seth said smiling through the annoyance in his tone. He obviously found a little humor in the situation, like a kid getting caught with his hand in the cookie jar. Tori was mortified.

"Millie sent me, Dean is look for her," Paige said a little snarky.

Oh no, Dean!

Tori felt a gut punch of guilt. What was she doing?

"I'm sorry Seth," she muttered "I have to go."

"See you later, beautiful," he said a little sad. Tori

made her way up the hill to where Paige impatiently waited for her, arms crossed. "Hey!" Seth suddenly yelled up after her. "Tomorrow, spears yeah?" He didn't wait for a response, he casually went back to target practice.

CHAPTER FIFTEEN

Dean

He was surrounded by darkness, choking on acrid smoke. He couldn't breathe, he couldn't see. The rocky ceilings above him felt close and the floor beneath him was cold. He sensed someone in the shadows not far away.

"Hey," Dean whispered. "Hey, where are we?" Dean reached out into the darkness and found a shape lying nearby. He crawled closer and grabbed the figure by the shoulder, which was sharp and angular. The person lying next to him was obviously very emaciated, their skin felt thin and papery under his fingers. Dean's eyes were adjusting to the light and he could make out the crumpled girl next to him. He carefully took her shoulder and rolled her over on her back, she was so frail he was afraid he may break one of her bones moving her. "Are you okay?" As he rolled her onto her back, her dark hair spilled from her face and Dean gasped. "Danielle?!"

Her face was broken and bloody, but it was his sister. He pulled her into his lap and shoved her chest to his ear listening for a heartbeat. He heard nothing. He saw now that her chest was sunken in completely on one side like her ribs had been beaten in severely. Her right arm bent in too many angles and her eyes were swollen completely shut.   She looked just as she had the day Dean had found her.

"No," Dean wept. "Not again."

Then, by some unseen force, Danielle was being pulled from Dean into the darkness. Dean frantically clung to his sister but he was suddenly bound by chains holding him back and Danielle was pried from his grip. Just as she slid into the shadows her eyes shot open, Dean strained against his chains watching in horrified, silence. Danielle opened her mouth and a scream more animal than human erupted from her lips. Dean watched in horror, tears pouring down his cheeks.

"Deeeeeeeeeeeean!   Help   meeeeeeeeeeeee!" Danielle shrieked as the darkness totally engulfed her.

That's when Dean began to scream.

When Dean opened his eyes a tiny red head was leaning over him, holding him gently to the bed. She was saying something to him, but he couldn't discern what she was saying over the sound of his own panic.

Where was Danielle? Oh god, they have Danielle!

The girl held fast to him, talking calmly. Wait, she wasn't talking. She was singing. The sweet melody broke through the panic first and his body settled down then he made out the words.

"The primrose in the sheltered rock

The crystal stream, the babbling brook
All these things, God's hands have made
For very love of thee
Twilight and shadows fall
Peace to his children all
Angles are guarding and they watch o'er thee
As you sleep
May angels watch over and may they guard o'er thee"

Dean's breath had calmed when he realized he was holding the girl's hand as she stroked his hair with the other.

"There you are," she smiled. "That was a bad one." She reached down and took a wet cloth from the water bowl on the floor near the bed. She wiped his forehead; he suddenly realized he was soaked in sweat. The cool water felt magnificent! "I'm Paige." She continued in silence for a minute, then said, "I used to get them too. They came for me too... It's terrible."

"How did you make it stop?" The raw sound of his voice surprised him and sounded foreign to his ears. Paige put the cloth back down in the dish and untied two leather straps she wore on each wrist revealing long, angry scars up her wrists.

"I tried to make everything stop." She looked down, "Apparently, the Caligo don't want cowards." She retied the leather cuffs. Dean watched in silence as the beautifully sad girl worked the leather between her fingers. She *was* beautiful. Her short hair gave way to a thin neck line and shoulders that Dean wanted to touch. Her eyes were a pale blue, not the piercing blue he had seen on Seth and Sari, but a quiet grey-blue that looked like the sea after a storm.

Suddenly the door opened and Millie burst into the room. She surveyed the scene.

"I heard him screaming from the river, is he all right?"

"He's okay now," Paige reassured her.

"Go fetch Tori; she'll want to know he's awake." Millie said as she came to Dean and checked his eyes and felt his head. Dean struggled to see around Millie's mothering gestures as Paige stood and started for the door.

"Wait," Dean grabbed her hand. "You're not a coward. And… you have the most beautiful voice I've ever heard." Paige smiled meekly then turned for the door. Dean watched her leave and knew… this was different.

Paige returned with Tori a few minutes later. The way that Tori and Paige regarded each other gave Dean the impression that Tori knew that something had passed between he and Paige. That they were somehow tethered to each other by that moment. Her song still played in his head. Tori sat stiffly at the end of the bed. She chewed on her thumb nail for a moment as an awkward silence stretch on.

"Are you okay?" She asked with genuine concern.

"Just… another nightmare." He looked over at Paige who stood silent near the doorway. "My sister was there." Tori's hand dropped and Millie turned to the conversation. "They had her. Is that even possible? She's dead!"

"They are baiting you," Paige said quietly.

"Paige, you don't have to be here for this," Millie said to her softly.

"No, I'm okay," Paige wiped her eyes. "I'm the only other one who has gone through this, and I might be able to help."

"They did this to you?" Tori asked Paige quietly, Paige only nodded. "I'm so sorry."

"Paige… helped me come out of it." Dean said tensely. Tori looked from Paige to Dean then back to Paige.

"Can you help him?"

"I don't know," Paige said, honestly.

"Well you helped him once right?" Tori pressed. Paige, again, nodded "Then try."

Paige agreed. Much to Dean's relief.

CHAPTER SIXTEEN

Allen

Why couldn't he have been born more athletic?

The archery lesson with Sari and her brother had been emasculating enough, but when Seth told him, with a smirk on his face, that Tori had hit the bull's eye on her second try, all remaining sense of manhood went out the window.

Thanks for sharing that Seth.

The wooden batons were also an epic failure. His knuckles were scraped and bloody and he was sure Sari was enjoying this a little too much, her giggles echoed across the gully. Seth's enthusiastic laughter at the scene didn't help either. Finally, exhausted he grabbed a nearby hatchet and threw it at the target. A bull's eye! Unfortunately Seth had missed it; Allen would have loved to see the shock on his face.

"So you're planning on carrying twenty or so hatchets in your belt at all times?" Sari taunted. "What do you do about the other nine or so Caligo who are running your way?"

"I plan on picking them up and tossing them outta my way… like this." He grabbed Sari by the waist and lifted her off the ground and over his shoulder. Sari squealed and kicked at him in mock terror.

Allen released his grip and let Sari slide down into his arms until they were face to face. Her perfect porcelain face was alight with laughter, making her eyes twinkle.

Now or never!

Allen pulled her lips to his; she was surprised but returned his kiss graciously. Something sparked as their lips touched and suddenly they were both hungry for one another. Sari's hands gripped the back of Allen's head, his hair threaded through her fingers as Allen wrapped his arms tighter around her small waist. Pulling her closer they stumbled backward into the trees, Allen catching them with an outstretched hand as they fell against the stalk of a flower-tree. Sari leaned bank against the tree and Allen leaned down kissing the edge of her cheek and neck then....

"Allen? Sari? You guys down here?"

Allen and Sari froze. They looked at each other, the spell of passion broken Sari began to laugh. Allen smiled and kissed her lightly on the lips before regaining his composure. Sari smoothed her hair, face flushed.

"Down here!" Allen called up.

Tori appeared around the corner, when she saw them and the heated looks on their faces her eyes grew wide with embarrassment.

"Oh... hey guys... Um... oh wow. I'm sorry." Tori laughed. "I can come back later."

Sari and Allen both laughed in embarrassment, Sari covered her face with her hands.

"It's okay T-bird, you're here. What's going on?" Allen could see Tori scrapping at the skin on the side of her thumb, her tell-tale nervous habit.

"I just wanted to talk to you. Oh my god, this is awkward," Tori laughed.

"That it is." Sari said, "I have to go do something anyway." She put a hand on Allen's arm. "I'll see you later?" Allen nodded. Sari said bye to Tori as she left and Tori returned a casual wave.

As soon as Sari was gone, Tori's mouth dropped open practically skipping over to Allen, slapping him on the arm.

"What was that?!"

"Don't start Miss Mood killer," Allen batted her away.

"I know. I'm sorry. But maybe next time try NOT being out in the middle of the gully in broad daylight?"

"So what do you want anyway?" Allen asked as he watched all the playfulness drain from his friend.

"Dean's nightmares aren't getting any better. This girl, Paige, it happened to her too and she is going to try to help but…"

"But what?"

"She isn't sure how much she can help," Tori began chewing her nails. "She didn't sound optimistic."

"So they are going to slowly drive him insane until..."

"Until he gets up and wanders up the mountain to them and they beat him, or enslave him or worse! And there is NOTHING we can do."

Just moments before, Allen had let himself forget the plight of their situation. There were serious problems they had to figure out: how to get home, how to stop the aging and most importantly, how to save Dean. Allen motioned for Tori to walk with him; they turned down the trail towards the river. They found the place Allen and Sari had sat and Allen led Tori to the boulder to sit.

"Wow, this is beautiful."

"Sari brought me down here. She showed me around a little."

"Seems weird huh?" Tori asked.

"What?"

"It seems like forever ago we were eating pizza in my kitchen and like that," Tori snapped her fingers, "everything changed."

"You're right. None of it seems quite real yet," Allen said thoughtfully.

"So you and Sari huh," Tori nudged his arm.

"I guess. Is that odd?" Allen asked. Tori laughed.

"Define 'odd' Allen! Look around! I think you

and Sari are the least 'odd' thing about this situation." Tori's honesty made Allen feel better, "How does it feel?"

"It feels… right." Allen finally concluded after searching for the right word.

"Well there ya go! That's all that matters," Tori smiled, then sighed heavily rubbing her face with her hands. Allen could see the conflict across her face.

"So Seth said you did really well with the bow," Allen steered the subject.

"Oh yeah?" Tori brightened a little, "What else did he say?" she asked quietly.

"That my aim sucked compared to yours!" Tori burst out laughing at this, sitting up a little straighter with pride. "What's going on T-bird?"

"I don't know," she whined, "he is so…." She obviously flushed. "Something. And there is Dean who is so sweet and I know I owe him for saving me especially if Beau really is here…" Allen turned sharply towards her.

"Tori you don't *owe* anyone anything!"

"But he got into a fight and didn't have to, not to mention that he wouldn't even be HERE if it wasn't for me!"

"So what?!" Allen almost yelled. He hated that Tori felt this way and put herself in these positions. He hated that she felt so small. "T-bird, I love you, but that has always been your issue. You stayed with Beau because you thought you had to fix him. You 'owed' him, too, remember? Dean stood up for you because he is a decent guy, but you shouldn't be with him because of some weird feeling of obligation." Allen took a deep breath, "Look, it's been less than a week. Just see what happens."

"But like you said…. It feels right." Tori said quietly.

"With Dean?"

"No."

Allen put his arm around his friend.

CHAPTER SEVENTEEN

Tori

Time passed in a blur.

Dean was finally able to get up and move around the village. Eloise followed him around excitedly, trotting after him wherever he went. Tori was introduced to the rest of the villagers and the enormous cows. Their giant wet noses dwarfed her hand but she liked them and let them nuzzle her. Dru had been butchering meat for the underground storage the day that Tori and Dean had ventured to the barn, the smell and site of the blood made Tori dizzy but Dean seemed riveted asking questions about the cut of the meant and how to keep the food edible without refrigeration. Tori tuned out and returned to the pasture to pet the huge grazing animals.

Dean and Tori had been spending more time together since his recuperation and her guilt about her encounter with Seth slowly subsided. Seth only coolly regarded her now with a nod or a smile when they passed in the village. Every time she saw him from across the village her stomach clenched with excitement, then faded quickly when he said nothing. She began to wonder if all the feelings she felt had been imagined. Maybe nothing had passed between them.

Dean's ribs were healing faster and it seemed as though the worst of the nightmares had passed. She would notice dark circles under his eyes when they met up in the mornings but within a couple hours he was back to his usual sweet self.

Allen and Sari were spending nearly all their time together. Allen was convinced they could find a way to get them all home and wanted to press Millie about what she was given to stop her aging. The age regression had come as a shock to Tori, but she had come to accept it as the reality with which she had to deal. Tori found herself staring at Millie and Sari's eyes at meals and during down time, looking at the subtle grey clouding and swirls around their eyes, it made her wonder if hers were beginning to darken as well.

Tori had taken up residence in a small cottage off by itself, Dean had objected at first but she had insisted on being alone. Millie had provided her with a comb made of bone and basic essentials to freshen herself up every day once she was settled, she still could not get used to washing from the small water basins. Tori's long hair had taken her hours to comb through; once it was silky in her hands again she twisted it in a long braid that nearly reached her waist. Tori liked the quiet of the Vale; at night even the sounds of the insects scurrying over the dome began to soothe her. At night she went to bed wishing she could talk to Seth. Wishing she didn't feel an obligation to Dean. Wishing she was stronger.

As Dean got stronger, he grew increasingly interested in Everidge's defenses and helping the villagers protect their home. Tori accompanied him to the gully one afternoon where Sari, Allen and Seth were already practicing. Seth and Sari were working on Allen's spear throwing, when he saw Tori and Dean come down the hill into the gully Allen groaned.

"Awesome. Now I have an audience," his words dripping with sarcasm. He turned back to the target and threw the spear, which missed… badly. Laughter exploded from Tori.

"T-bird, seriously that is not helping," Allen said over his shoulder. Tori clasped her hands over her mouth and tried to contain herself.

"Why don't you show him how it's done?" Seth said to Tori, much to her amazement since he hadn't talked to her in weeks. He walked around Allen and handed her a bow and the quiver of arrows. Tori's heart quickened pace. The sound of his voice after so long of silence gave her a jolt of glee through her stomach.

"Okay," she said reaching for the bow, but Dean took it instead. Dean regarded her as if she were as fragile as a china doll.

"You sure?" Dean asked her, not meaning to be

condescending or embarrass her, but he had succeeded at both. Tori's face got hot with embarrassment, she looked around at the faces all staring at her and she felt anger starting to rise. She looked at Seth, whose expression was furious.

"She's got it, mate." Seth jerked the bow from Dean and stepped around him to Tori in one fluid motion. Tori's hands trembled. As Seth put the bow in her hand he stroked her hand with his thumb, in a hidden gesture of reassurance. He squeezed her hand then backed away. Tori looked down at the bow, fuming from the inside out. Seth believed she could do, why didn't Dean? Why would he? She had let herself become this delicate thing to be cared for. A wave of calm rushed over her. "Show 'em, yeah?" Seth smiled. Tori nodded.

Tori walked quickly to the line etched deep into the ground, Allen withdrew next to Sari who had been quietly watching the whole exchange. She loaded her arrow and quicker than she knew she was capable of doing she pulled back, focused and (breathe) released.

Thunk!

She hit the target dead center.

Her heart pounded victoriously as she turned and shoved the bow back at Seth as Dean still stood back staring at her. She glared at Dean and marched over to him, meeting him face to face. She stared him in the eye and quietly declared.

"I don't need rescuing anymore,"

Dean said nothing and before he could, Tori stormed off up the rise pushing past Paige who had silently been watching from the sidelines. Tori hadn't even known she was there.

"Excuse me," she mumbled as she passed the girl.

She stomped down the trail toward the river. Her heart still pounded furiously when she reached the boulder bench but she was too irritated to sit so she paced. She realized then that she hadn't felt anger in a long time; she hadn't felt ANYTHING in a long time. She was a robot just moving along from day to day. Now she felt *alive!* The last time she felt even remotely alive was before her dad died. She was mad at her dad for leaving. She was mad at her dad for dying before she could know him. She was mad at her mom for building a wall between then so she didn't ever get hurt again. She was mad that her mom had left her alone, so Tori had put herself to sleep.

She walked around like a zombie for years... YEARS.... Because anger was no way to exist. But neither was this! She would *never* need rescuing again. The trees rustled behind her and she spun expecting to see Dean, but when Seth came around the bend a fresh flow of anger pumped through her veins.

"I am *not* weak" She screamed at him.

"I know," he said quietly.

"I am in this backward-ass world with no way home, oh and let's not forget the psycho ex-boyfriend of mine who freaking *followed* me here! I *can't* be asleep anymore!" She paced as she continued to fume at Seth.

"Okay," He said calmly, letting her get it out

"That is no way to live!"

"No it isn't," he said patiently.

"And you!" she pointed at Seth, turning the rant on him personally. "You and I have this… this moment and then NOTHING! Something happened in that gully between us, and you said what you said, then you say NOTHING to me! NOTHING! What am I supposed to…" Seth closed the distance between them in two steps, cupping her face and bringing her lips to his. Tori was caught off guard, the rage melting away instantly but she returned his kiss eagerly. Seth pulled back but kept his face close to Tori's.

"I'm sorry," Seth breathed. "I didn't know what to say to you. And the whole thing with Dean… I didn't know how…" He leaned his forehead against hers.

"You could've started with 'Hi'" Tori said, Seth broke into laughter and kissed her again softly on the lips. They let their hands fall between them, fingers intertwined.

A branch snapped behind them making them

both jump and turn to see Paige standing in the trail glowering at them both, shaking her head.

"Dean wanted me to check on you, but I can see Seth has that all under control." With a hard look she turned and headed back up the trail. Tori rolled her eyes and followed her.

CHAPTER EIGHTEEN

Dean

Paige came rushing back up the path, anger flushing her face.

"Where's Tori?" He asked as she passed him in a huff.

"Ask HIM!" She shouted continuing across the village. Dean looked back at the trail confused as Tori and Seth emerged. Were they holding hands? Dean stormed toward Seth and with a hand to his chest, pushed Seth backward a foot or two (even with the height and weight advantage Seth had on him). Seth recovered quickly.

"Oh, you're feelin' better mate?" He said coming at Dean full force. Allen and Sari ran and intercepted them before they could collide and struggled to separate them.

"Dean! Calm down!" Allen said wrestling with him.

"Seth! Back off!" Sari was struggling to contain her brother.

"ENOUGH!" Tori burst into the fray and pushed the boys apart on either side of her. Dean's adrenaline pumped furiously but at the sight of Tori standing between them he backed off and shook Allen off of him.

"I'm good!" Dean held his hands up, and looked directly at Tori. "I'm done." He threw Seth an intimidating glare then turned and left.

He heard Tori following after him, yelling his name, but he ignored her until he got to the threshold of his cabin. He threw open the door and spun to meet Tori, who nearly skidded to a stop.

"I know you don't need rescuing!" He shouted at her, "I know you have fight in you Tori! I can see it! I saw it the first time I laid eyes on you!" Tori stared at him for a minute.

"Then why…."

"The bow?" Dean laughed, "Better question," he took a step toward her and stared down at her hard in anger. "What did you think you had to prove?" With that he went inside and slammed the door before he said something he might regret.

CHAPTER NINETEEN

Tori

Millie had decided Tori needed something other than Seth and Dean to focus on, so she dragged her down to the large cottage at the center of the village where a large earth oven burned almost all the time. This cottage was two stories and built into the girth of a flower-tree A shaded pavilion jutted out from it, creating a shaded porch area lined with a wooden railing which was topped with flat stone counter tops. Madelyn sat at the counter kneading bread, she smiled warmly at Tori. While further down the in the pavilion, secluded in the shade, Paige was grinding something with a large mortar and pestle.

"Madalyn and Paige will show you what needs to be done," Millie said as she scurried away.

Great… Tori thought as Paige shot daggers at her from across the porch.

"Here, take this dough and knead it until its smooth then we will pop it in the oven," Madalyn said cheerfully. Tori took a bowl of cream colored dough from her and sat herself down at the counter. The oven was seated in the base of the flower-tree, which they used as a chimney as smoke trails drifted from an opening at the top of the trunk.

After several quiet minutes of the girls tending to their work, Madalyn could no longer contain herself.

"So I heard there was quite a ruckus between Dean and Seth."

"Yes there was. Just guys blowing off steam, ya know?" Tori said politely.

Paige scoffed from her corner.

"What happened?" Madalyn asked, eager for more details. Madalyn was a gossip junkie looking for a fix.

"Just, something stupid that got out of hand," Tori said, praying this conversation would end.

"No," Paige spoke up loudly suddenly. "What happened is that *Princess* here is too good for some things."

Tori turned toward Paige, honestly shocked. She didn't think she was better than ANYONE. She was scared of everything!

"What?! That's not true at all," Tori protested.

"Really? Because I have seen Dean be nothing but pretty damn protective of you and you threw it in his face in front of everyone!" Paige ground harder in whatever she had in the stone bowl.

Probably grinding up something to poison me with.

"Look, I just don't want to be defended or rescued anymore." Tori spoke softly hoping to diffuse the situation. Paige stopped grinding and glared at Tori.

"Spoken like someone who's always HAD protection!" Paige nearly screamed at her slamming the stone bowl down on the wood table in front of her and stood. "Some people NEED rescuing, Princess, and they NEVER get it!" She stomped out from the shade of the porch and into the sunlight when she stopped and turned. "But don't worry," Paige said coldly "Once Dean finds out about you and Seth, you won't have to worry about his pesky protection anymore!" She was seething at Tori when it finally occurred to Tori why Paige hated her so much.

"Are you in love with Dean?" Tori blurted out. Paige's eyes widened in surprise and Tori knew she had hit the nail on the head.

"You don't deserve him," Paige muttered before turning and walking out of sight.

Tori didn't deserve him. He deserved someone who *wanted* to be with him, not someone who felt like they had to. But Tori was beginning to realize that she deserved that too. She knew that Dean and Paige were close, but hadn't seen it until now how Paige felt about him. If she really cared about Dean, wouldn't she have picked up on that?

"Don't take Paige too seriously," Madalyn said quietly. "She's been through a lot. She's just…. Lost"

Tori worked through the afternoon as Madalyn chipperly talked away about how she ended up in Everidge (she was out walking her dog when "Oh! What is that?"), how long she had been there (three years, two months and ten days) and how she felt so much more useful here than back home ("I just figure, 'Gosh, this all must have happened for a reason!'")

Dear God, did she ever shut up?

Tori nodded politely and said "Mm hmm" at all the appropriate places but her mind was elsewhere. Once they had worked through the barrel full of dough and Tori's hands were almost too cramped to move them, Madalyn slipped all the loaves in the giant oven with Tori's help.

"You have some first class love drama to attend to. Have fun for me!" Madalyn said as she waved goodbye. Tori decided to go see Dean. She owed him at least an explanation for what was going on. It wasn't as if she'd known Dean long enough for them to be exclusive, but she felt *something* for him. Maybe not the electric, all-consuming feeling she had for Seth but she respected Dean and she felt a sweet fondness for him. Was that enough?

"Enough for what?" she said aloud. She looked around self-consciously making sure no one heard her talking to herself. The only person was Roth, who was busy chopping wood and simply waved in her direction.

Why did it need to be anything?

Tori approached Dean's house apprehensively but made herself lift her hand to knock. Before she could rap the door it swung open abruptly, startling Tori back a little. Dean stood in the doorway wide-eyed; Tori could see something was off.

"Dean?" Tori asked, but he didn't respond. He walked past her out into the day. "Hey, Dean?" Tori rushed to his side and grabbed his arm to slow his stride, when she did this he grabbed her forcefully and threw her to the side continuing his walk without a second glance at her. It suddenly hit her what was happening, he was leaving. "Dean!" she screamed. "Roth! Help!" She risked a second assault on him and threw herself on Dean's back. Roth came running, shouting for more help.

"We've got a walker!" Roth yelled as he wrapped his huge arms around Dean trying to immobilize him. Tori slid down off of Dean's back and took handfuls of Dean's shirt digging her heels into the ground but was still pulled along helplessly as Dean trudged against her and Roth. Paige appeared first and, without hesitation, joined Tori pulling him backwards, both girls finally wrapping their arms around his waist for better leverage. Seth came out of nowhere and he and Roth finally were able to stop Dean's progress, the fact that the two muscular men struggled to keep Dean still was horrifying. Sari and Allen appeared with rope and chains, Dru close behind.

"Just try to keep him steady," Dru said.

As the group closed in tighter around Dean, he continued to struggle like a man walking in hardening concrete. He didn't fight them or attempt to swing on them, he just pressed ever forward, in slow, straining footsteps. Dru struggled to secure the rope around Dean's calves, but the ropes automatically tangled and fell. Finally Roth grabbed one loose end of the rope, pulling it tight while Dru tied the ends together. Dean's legs buckled and he fell to the ground. Dru and Roth quickly took hold of his top half and secured him with the chains.

Everyone fell back in silence.

Dean groaned and began to stir. His eyes finally focused on the world around him and looked down at the ropes and chains.

"Hey, what… What the hell?" He said as he struggled against the chains. A sigh exploded from Tori and she rushed to his side

"Dean! You scared me!" she threw her arms around his neck, just thankful he was okay. Tori heard the grit of gravel under foot behind her and turned to see Seth walking away.

*   *   *

That night Tori couldn't sleep.

Her mind spun and her heart was torn. She kept replaying Dean's "walker" episode followed instantly by the look of hurt on Seth's face before he simply left. He just walked away. That hurt the most.

She couldn't help it that she cared about Dean and she couldn't help it that she cared about Seth. The way she cared about them was incomparable, but she didn't know how to tell either one of them that. The only thing worse than this, was KNOWING she should be more concerned about getting home. In a weird way though, she liked Everidge. She wasn't constrained by her old life where she was always scared and compliant. Here she had possibilities. She was stronger and felt more alive here.

Outside the wind whipped the limbs of the trees and flowers around her cottage. Her shutters were open to let the cool air in, but a ghostly sound soon drifted through as well. She sat up, sitting perfectly still, straining to hear the noise that tickled her ear moments earlier. Just when she was about to lie back down with the assumption she was going crazy, she heard it again.

The howl of a wolf. She went to the end of her bed and leaned to the window trying to find the source of the sound. It sounded close. Tori knew Dru had a "pet" wolf down in the barn, but she was still a baby and Tori had never heard her howl.

A thick fog had rolled in, weaving in around the trees and flower stalks into the village, slithering through the dome. The fog moved with purpose and Tori strained to look out the window to watch it spread as it slithered into the village clearing. It spread its ghostly fingers wide reaching out to all corners of the village. Tori looked down and saw misty trails, seeping up the side of her house, sending her scrambling backwards as it poured in through her window. Tori jumped from her bed and headed for the door, fog rolled in under the door trapping her. She backed away from the door and the window into the corner of the room, the fog closing in on her from three sides. Her heart was pounding and as the fog licked her skin, her eyes began to water and her lungs began to sting. She coughed and her vision began to double. She tried to scream but she couldn't get enough air. Her arms and legs felt like dead weight, numb and useless. Unable to control her muscles any longer she fell forward onto the floor, letting the spreading numbness take over her body.

As the world grew dark she heard the howl once more.

CHAPTER TWENTY

Allen

His head felt like it was going to split open.

For a few minutes he struggled to remember where he was or what was going on.

Then it slowly came back to him.

He and Sari had been kissing. Something had interrupted them. They heard something… A howl. They had looked out the window and had seen something… The fog.

Allen's eyes snapped open as he remembered Sari struggling to breath and how his body had gone limp and he couldn't get to her. He was half on his bed as he looked around for Sari who was crumpled on the floor a foot or so away from him. She was just beginning to stir. Allen moved off the bed and slid next to her on the floor, helping her sit up. She swayed a little and looked like she might be sick.

"Stay still," Allen stood and on unsteady legs, staggered across the room to the water basin. He sloppily threw a nearby rag into the water and rang the water out of it again. He returned to Sari falling heavily onto his knees. "Here," he put the rag on the back of Sari's neck then lay down on the floor next to her, trying to stop the world from spinning.

"What happened?" Allen mumbled.

"Poison fog," Sari said, still very groggily. "The scavs send it, they make it or something."

"Why?" Allen rolled on to his side letting his cheek rest on the cool stone floor.

"To take someone…" Sari sighed in realization, "Oh no!"

"Dean."

*   *   *

The debilitating effects of the fog took almost an hour to wear off, though Allen's head still throbbed, he and Sari made their way to Dean's cottage where their fears were confirmed. Millie was already inside staring sadly at the empty bed. She looked up at Sari with glassy eyes.

"I should've stayed with him," She said as she began to weep.

"Millie it's not your fault…" Sari began but Tori suddenly burst into the doorway. Her face was ashen and her eyes bloodshot.

"No…" she whispered. She leaned against the doorframe.

"T," Allen said sympathetically.

"This is all my fault," Tori said beginning to cry.

Sari went to her then. Taking Tori by the arms and leaning her against her shoulder.

"Tori, this is not your fault." The way Sari regarded his friend, warmed Allen's heart. He was falling for this beautiful girl and wasn't sure where that road led. "Lucius was targeting him; it had nothing to do with you."

"But I'm the whole reason he is even here!" Tori cried. "Maybe, if I had been here…"

"Then they would've taken you too," Seth said as he came up behind Tori who looked up at him with such an agonized expression, it almost broke Allen's heart. Without a word she turned and ran from the cottage.

Seth and Allen had spent the afternoon fixing the hole left in the dome from the Caligo kidnappers. Seth hadn't said much, which had been great for Allen because when Seth did speak it was usually to mock Allen, but today he was different. Seth showed Allen which vines to cut and how to weave them securely into the thatching and Allen, surprisingly, didn't suck at it. As they finished up and returned from the village Seth was quiet, in deep thought.

"You know Tori has never really known where she belongs. Or with whom." Allen said. Seth didn't say anything but he was listening. "Except for me, she's always been alone. Her dad left, then died. Then her mom left her basically alone to fend for herself, for months at a time. Everyone she has ever relied on has left and she can't see that only a strong person can survive that. I don't know what's going between you two, and frankly it's so complicated I might not want to know, but what I do know is that she has never felt strong, until you helped her to feel strong." Allen stopped and looked at Seth seriously. "You don't want to be with her, fine. But don't let her give up on that." Seth nodded and they continued through the village in silence.

Everyone gathered at the pavilion of the large cottage a few hours later. After the late night attack, everyone was feeling shaky and vulnerable. Their slim illusion of security had been shattered, and not for the first time.

"So what do we do now?" Allen asked Millie, who was trying to calm everyone.

"Unfortunately, there's not much we can do."

"What?!" Tori exclaimed. "We can't just leave him there! This shouldn't have happened in the first place! His nightmares had stopped! Why did they even come for him?"

"His nightmares never stopped," Paige said quietly. "They were getting worse, he just didn't want anyone to know." Tori was quiet again and a hush fell over everyone.

"Well regardless of that, we can't just abandon

him. You guys have rescued others, right?" Allen said looking around the small group of faces. Sari shifted uncomfortably next to him.

"Allen, it's not that simple. We have rescued our people, but we always lose so many in doing so. Look around. There are barely any of us left." Sari waved her around over the group.

"What about Millie?" Allen asked, "How did she get free?" Everyone was silent.

"They let me go," Millie finally said after a few moments.

Everyone, including Sari, seemed shocked by this.

"Millie, you never told me that."

"I know love; there is a lot I haven't told you." Millie took a deep breath, "They took me the same way they took Dean, in the middle of the night after months of tortuous nightmares. When I woke up I was in a dungeon chained to wall. It was so hot inside the mountain. They made us all work in the mines until we dropped then... well then they would take the bodies away. When I burnt my hands I thought they were done with me, but instead of taking me to their butcher, they took me to their alchemist. He had hundreds of potions in a cabinet; he gave me what they called Dragon Tears. It was a bitter tasting blue gel, they forced it down my throat but it healed my hands. They seemed to know something I didn't, but the next thing I knew I was free."

Millie took a deep breath. "Once I was home though I realized over time that my aging had stopped and I was more connected with the Caligo."

"What do you mean Millie?" Sari asked suspiciously.

"I can sense… almost see when the Portis is opening. And…" Millie hesitated, "Sometimes I can see what the Caligo see, where they are, what they are doing. I never said anything because it frightened me, and I didn't want to frighten anyone else."

"What?!" Sari yelled, everyone stirring with agitation.

"It's not all the time! Just sometimes when I am falling asleep or off guard, I get flashes."

"Did you get any 'flashes' last night?!" Tori said accusingly, from beside Allen.

"Yes," Millie looking down in shame. The crowd roared at this, a thousand questions and accusations flying at her at the same time. Sari stood from her seat and walked to the front of the pavilion next to Millie. Everyone grew quiet again.

"Every time we lost someone, did you know before?" Sari's porcelain face was flushed with anger; Allen could feel the sizzle of tension in the air.

"I… I wasn't sure."

"Millie!" Madalyn gasped. Roth stood and

stormed off across the village. Sari took a step toward Millie and addressed her harshly.

"So you LET them take Natalie! We nearly lost Roth because of it! They tormented Paige until she slit her bloody *wrists!*" Allen and Tori both looked at Paige in shock, who dropped her eyes in shame. "And now they've taken Dean!" Sari screamed.

"I'm sorry... I was so afraid," Millie said tears coming to her eyes.

"Afraid?" Tori burst out, "I've been 'afraid' since the minute we got here and I had to face it!" Allen grabbed her arm as she rose from her seat to speak, which she promptly pulled away. "And now Dean is gone and we find out you could have prevented it! You're a coward!" Tori's words spit out like venom.

"Tori!" Allen hissed but Tori was already leaving. She pushed past Seth who after a few seconds followed her.

Sari let the tension settle in the crowd then got everyone's attention.

"Everybody listen up! We're going on a rescue mission!"

Yeah... Allen loved that girl.

They sent Madalyn to retrieve Roth who returned begrudgingly, refusing to look at Millie. They left Tori and Seth alone for now at Allen's suggestion. Her new fondness for being a hot head was not going to help this situation any. Millie was tasked with writing down everything she could remember about the mountain, including a map of the tunnels inside. Annie and Dru were sent to Everidge's underground weapon storage bunker which, from Allen's understanding, was actually more of a hole. They would also fashion any new weapons that were needed to help storm the mountain. And by the time that Allen was helping Roth bring down the dome, they had the start of a plan to rescue Dean.

Sari and Allen excused themselves from everyone after dinner had been served and sat side by side near the dome overlooking the field of fireflies. They settled in the grass, leaning back against an apple tree. Sari was very quiet, twirling a lock of her hair deep in thought.

"You okay?" Allen asked her.

"Yeah, just thinking...." She took Allen's hand and intertwined her fingers with his. "This helps," she smiled. The flashing lights of the fireflies illuminated her eyes in waves of blue-green splendor. Allen's heart beat faster just looking at her. He leaned over and kissed her softly, cupping her face in his hand. Soon soft kisses turned into fierce passion. He had never felt this need, this want, this... love before. And he knew in the way Sari returned his kisses that she felt it too.

In the lights of the fireflies Allen whispered, "I love you."

"I love you, too," Sari whispered.

CHAPTER TWENTY-ONE

Tori

After leaving the meeting at the pavilion, Seth had caught up with Tori and had taken her back to his cottage, which was basically just a house built into a cave at the edge of the village. Despite the coolness of the stone walls, his home was warm and well lived in. Tori sat down by the fire while Seth set about making her some tea, it was strange watching Seth doing such a domestic and delicate task. It felt intimate to Tori. He hung the teapot on a hook above the fire then sat down across from her.

"I shouldn't have yelled at Millie," Tori said miserably. Seth waved a hand at her.

"You're cute when you get mad," he smiled. Tori glared at him, so he raised his hands in submission. "Sorry, not helpful."

"I should've been there." At that, Seth's smile faded. He shook his head and leaned forward.

"And what would you have done? They use the poison fog for a reason, yeah?" He carefully took her hand. Tears began to well in Tori's eyes.

"I don't know," she swiped at her tears angrily.

"Tori… If you would've been taken, I don't know what I would've done. I can't take on a mountain full of Caligos by myself but, I sure would've tried."

"Why me? I'm such a mess!" Tori laughed.

"Well look at you," Seth said trying to lighten the mood. "Who wouldn't fall in love with you?" Seth stopped short. Tori's heartbeat quickened.

"What did you say?" Tori could barely breathe. Seth let out an embarrassed laughed, rubbing his hand on the back of his neck.

"I said I love you," He said looking her in the eye. "From the moment I saw you at the Portis I knew. I had told myself I was fine being alone, but when I saw you… I needed you. Lucky me when I found out you needed me, too." Tori laughed with tears streaming down her cheeks. She leaned over and kissed him tenderly.

"I do need you! I'm sorry. I'm so sorry for every confusing thing I've done to you. You saved me from being trapped inside myself forever! I needed you to help find *me* and I can never, repay you for that." Seth kissed her again pulling her onto his lap.

"Well, we'll work on that later." He smiled, kissing her again but Tori stopped.

"Seth, we have to get Dean out of there. I don't feel for him what I feel for you, but he *did* save me once, and he wouldn't be here if it wasn't for me. I have to make this right." Tori pleaded. Seth looked down towards the fire and considered this; he looked up again with little hesitation.

"Well, then we've got work to do." Surprised, Tori slipped from his lap onto her feet as he stood. "We can't very well leave Dean up there having all the fun." Seth grabbed his bow from a peg by the door and wrapped a leather belt, fitted with a sheath and knife around his waist. When he turned towards Tori again she threw herself into his strong arms, kissing him.

"Thank you," she whispered.

"Yeah, yeah. I'm a great guy. Let's go." He smiled as he opened the door for her and they headed out toward the gully.

The brilliant light of sunset was creeping into the edges of the horizon as they began setting up the targets around the gully. Seth positioned Tori at the line in the center of the targets, with one in front of her, to the left, right and behind her.

"Okay, shoot what's in front of you first." Tori did as she was told and nailed an arrow in the middle of the front target, she reseated another arrow and as she stretched back the string Seth stepped up behind her. With his hand on the base of her back and guiding hand on her left bicep he whispered in her ear, "Swing your whole body to the next target," she felt his breath on her ear making her heart beat faster. She swung right and let her arrow fly.

Thunk!

Bull's eye! With his lips still at her ear he whispered, "Again."

She swung left and released it. As the tell-tale *Thunk!* echoed off the trees, she spun free of Seth's hand, reseating another arrow and aimed at the last target behind Seth. Seth wasn't quick enough and stood stunned momentarily between Tori's arrow and the target. Tori smiled triumphantly, Seth nodded in approval but suddenly ducked around her bow knocking it out of her hands, tumbling with Tori to the ground.

"Okay, now what do you do?" Tori struggled underneath him but he was immovable. Seth smiled, devilishly, egging her on. Tori felt a surge of panic rush through her, familiar and terrible. She focused on Seth, his eyes and his voice. He sensed her fear and eased up a little.

"Tori, you can't lose control. When you panic, you put yourself in real danger. I'm right here." Seth talked easy and Tori became grounded once more, beating back the panic into submission.

Tori reached down to Seth's waistband, his eyes widened in surprise knocking him temporarily off balance. This gave Tori just enough time to unsheathe the knife in his belt and bring it to his throat.

"I do this!" Tori's heart slammed against her chest but she felt strong and exhilarated.

"Nice job," Seth said keeping his chin up and neck very still. Tori lowered the blade and threw it aside, wrapping her arms around his neck and kissing him. Seth leaned into her but then pulled back breathless.

"I like where your head's at," he kissed her once more quickly on the lips. "But we aren't done yet." He stood then held is hand out for Tori to take and helped her up. "Let's do it again." Seth picked his knife up off the ground and threw it across the gully at the center target, the blade sticking squarely in the center ring.

Wow, Tori thought

"Show me how to do that!"

CHAPTER TWENTY-TWO

Dean

It was so dark.

Dean was strapped, arms outstretched on either side of him to the cold stone wall. He didn't know how long he had been there but the screaming pain in his shoulders told him at least few days. His throat was dry, he could barely swallow and the emptiness in his stomach sent spastic cramps through his abdomen.

From somewhere in the darkness he heard the gritting sound of boots against stone. He strained his eyes against the darkness desperately trying to make out any form in the dark but could make out nothing. The unseen figure came closer, so close Dean could smell him. After a few tense moments, too close for comfort, the figure backed away and seemed to settle against the opposite wall.

"So here we are," a voice slithered out of the darkness, but Dean did not reply

"What's the matter, don't recognize my voice Pretty Boy?"

No… Not him.

"Beau," Dean steadied his quivering voice.

"That's right," Beau replied. Dean heard the scrape of a flint and then the room was lit with burning torchlight. Dean's eyes shut against the sudden, piercing light. "Oh, too bright, Pretty Boy?" Beau stepped closer and pain exploded in his left leg, his nostrils filling with the smell of burning flesh. Dean screamed in pain opening his eyes. Beau was inches from his face, torch still in hand.

"Wh…. What the happened to you?" Dean said in horror as he stared at the monster Beau had become. Beau's forehead protruded fiercely outward, his jaw and cheek bones jutted out stretching his skin so that it looked that it might rip from his bones. He had grown enormous, with sickeningly big muscles rippling his 7 foot frame.

"You like it?" he grinned, doing a turn for Dean. "Lucius gave me some upgrades… And my first play thing."

"You *let* them turn you into this?! You can't be that crazy!" Dean said, desperately. Beau smiled revealing his gleaming row of sharp teeth.

"You have no idea what I'm capable of."

CHAPTER TWENTY-THREE

Sari

Allen was still sleeping when Sari woke with the sun the next morning. The grass was freezing against her skin; she reached across Allen and grabbed her tunic. She looked down at him and smiled as he began to wake. The night before ran through her head a shiver of joy ran through her body, making her smile. She traced the curve of his cheek with her finger then brushed some of his dirty blonde hair off his forehead where she leaned in and kissed him lightly.(I think for the intended age, we should remove the innuendo here...)

"Allen," she whispered "it's freezing, let's get inside." He opened his eyes and smiled when he saw her.

"Good morning," he lifted his head off the ground looking at their surroundings and laughed. "Wow..." was all he managed to say with a laugh.

"Come on," Sari grabbed his arm and pulled him off the ground. He was still shirtless, though shivering a bit, he was strong but not over muscular. Sari trailed her finger down his chest absentmindedly.

"We could stay a little bit," Allen said wrapping his arms around her waist. She laughed pushing him away.

"We *need* to go. You want Seth or Roth to find us here, like *this?*"

"No, I've embarrassed myself enough in front of those two" Allen said shaking his shirt on, groaning at the feel of the cold fabric.

"Besides, we have a lot to do if we are going to rescue Dean with any success." Sari threw her cloak over her should then looked around the tree to see if anyone was coming. "Okay, let's go."

"Has there ever been a SUCCESSFUL rescue? You said yesterday that every time you rescue someone, you lose far more than are rescued. There aren't many of us right now to begin with." Allen pointed out.

The last rescue mission hadn't gone well. Natalie had been taken much the same way Dean had. Roth had been incapacitated by the fog as he slept next to her. They had met after Natalie came through the Portis and fell in love almost instantly, Roth loved her fiercely. He blamed himself for not being strong enough to withstand the effects of the fog.

They had put a rescue party together in haste and stormed the mountain's only entrance only to be met with force. The Caligo rained down upon them with ferocity. The villagers meager weapons were no match for the iron forged swords and maces the Caligo wielded. A man named Marcus was cut in half. Seth had taken an arrow to the leg and, just before Sari screamed the call of retreat, Roth made a break for the cave opening where

Lucius was waiting, an enormous mass of muscle and evil.

The Caligo all shared the same jutted jaws which perfectly displayed their horrifying teeth. They hand an extra set of canine teeth on both the top and bottom that stood taller and sharper than the rest. Their noses flared at the scent of the dying. They stood 8 feet tall or so with rounded muscular shoulders and arms.

But Lucius dwarfed them all. He was monstrous.

Sari watched in horror as Lucius lifted Roth off the ground by his neck. Roth kicked and fought against the enormous creature but was simply outmatched. Lucius seemed to study his reaction with amusement, but then he very slowly, pushed his sword through Roth's midsection.

Sari had her bow armed and focused before she knew what she was doing; she released the arrow striking Lucius in his right shoulder. He dropped Roth who crumpled to the ground unmoving, but Lucius was now focused on Sari.

Sari screamed for a retreat as she ran for the cave yelling for Dru who joined her, battling away Caligo rangers along the way. They reached the mouth of the cave, Sari ready with an armed bow aimed at Lucius' head.

"Let us take him," she demanded in a shaking

voice. Lucius regarded her with humor but he also seemed interested in these small creatures who dared attack his fortress. Like rats in a lab.

"You are out-matched little one," his voice was as deep as thunder and reverberated through her.

"It would seem so," she shook from head to toe but never lost her aim.

"You call yourself warriors? Warriors do not retreat!" he boomed at her.

"We aren't warriors! We are just people. You took one of ours and we want her back!" Sari screamed.

"Ah… the female…." Lucius waved to someone in the depths of the cave who came forward dragging a terrified Natalie. Roth screamed her name, and then sunk to the ground again from the pain. Dru lowered his spear and helped to steady Roth. "This is the one you seek?"

"Yes, let us have her and we will leave. There is no reason for us to fight one another." Sari said, suddenly hopeful they would make it out alive with Natalie. Her optimism was short lived.

Lucius threw his horned head back and laughed, shaking the ground.

"There will never be peace between us." He swung his sword and struck Natalie dead. Sari heard nothing now over Roth's screaming. Blinded by horror

Sari let her arrow fly striking Lucius in his left eye. Sari spun and grabbed Roth's arm.

"Dru! Help me!" She shouted over Roth's agonizing screams. They dragged Roth into the valley where the rest of the villagers waited. Sari and Millie had been able to save Roth and stitch up Seth's leg but no one talked about had happened for days. Dru and Sari, never spoke of what they witnessed again. Millie sat with Roth through the worst of his depression and recuperation until he was healed enough to carry on.

Suddenly, Sari realized the advantage they had over the Caligo.

Millie.

"I need to find Millie!" Sari said excitedly to Allen, breaking into a run across the village.

Sari quickly made her way across the village to Millie's cottage and knocked quickly on her door, waiting until Millie opened the door. She was obviously surprised to see her. Sari had known Millie for years and she resisted the urge to grab her and hug her.

"Can we talk Millie?" She only nodded, stepping aside to let Sari inside where she seated herself at the table.

"I need to know everything you remember about your time in the mountain."

Millie sat down and thought carefully. Then

reached across her small wooden table and took the map she had sketched the day before.

"The mines were at the heart of the mountain, here. A cluster of smaller tunnels branched off the central passage that opens at the mouth of the cave. What are you thinking?"

"That perhaps there is something you saw that could help us. Are you sure there is only one way into the mountain? We can't go in by the front door, we were slaughtered last time."

"I know dear, I'm so sorry," Millie said, choked with tears. Sari reached across the table and took her hand.

"Millie, that is behind us. What is in front of us is a rescue where more people could die. Please, think." Sari said kindly but in earnest.

"That's all I can remember, I'm sorry. Aside from their ceremonies…." Millie stopped short and stood up so fast she nearly knocked her chair over. "Wait!" she ran to her book shelf and grabbed a leather scroll from the shelf and hurried back to the table. "The moon!"

Sari was confused. "What the bloody hell are you talking about, Millie?"

Millie spread the rolled leather out onto the table over the map to reveal a lunar chart.

"The blood moon!" Millie proclaimed proudly.

"The Caligo have a Blood Moon Ceremony!"

"So what does that mean for us?"

"Every…" Millie rearranged the maps again, putting the map of the mountain next to the lunar chart, parts of each draping over the side of the small table top. "Every blood moon they would all gather in the central passage and go out a back passage that was only opened on the night of their Blood Moon Ceremony." She traced a path with her finger down the main passage and to the back slope of the mountain where she drew an X.

"There's a back entrance?! They have no idea we know about this!" Sari stood in excitement. "When is the next blood moon?" Sari asked quickly. Millie ran her finger across the leather bound lunar chart and thought quietly for a moment.

"Sixty-two days," Millie said gravely.

"Sixty-two days…." Sari sat back down. "We can't leave him there that long. He won't make it."

"It's the only chance you'll have to have the element of surprise." Millie sympathized.

"I need to talk to the others," Sari gathered the leather scroll and the map and turned to leave. She stopped and returned wrapping her free arm around Millie. "Thank you."

Sari found Allen and Tori eating breakfast under the shade of large weeping pear tree, she also spied

Paige sitting alone closer to the pavilion. Ever since her "accident" Sari kept a watchful eye on her. As she approached them the smell of the beef hash and oats they were eating hit Sari's nose and made bile turn in her stomach. A wave of nausea passed over her, making her knees weak.

"Hey Sari," Tori said smiling, but her soon smiled faded when she saw Sari's face. "Are you okay? You look pale."

"I'm fine darling, thank you." She waved off Tori's concern then sat next to Allen. "I just spoke with Millie," she paused and called Paige over. "She needs to hear this too," she said to Tori, who agreed without hesitation. After Paige sat down awkwardly next to Tori, Sari continued, "There is another way into the mountain and the Caligo don't know we know it exists." They all perked at this news.

"There is a slight drawback."

"Of course there is," Tori groaned. Allen smacked her in the arm shushing her.

"I need to know how you guys feel about it before we decide what to do," Sari said carefully.

"What's the catch Sari?" Allen asked.

"The other way into the mountain won't be open until the next blood moon."

"And when is that?" Paige asked.

"Sixty-two days," Sari said flatly.

"WHAT?!" Paige shouted, leaping to her feet. "You can't leave him there that long, Sari, you CAN'T!" Paige cried, desperation raging in her eyes.

Sari stood and put a hand on the girl's slender shoulder. "Paige it's the only way to avoid a slaughter. If you want to save Dean, than you need to be patient." Paige's eyes frantically darted from Sari, to Allen then to Tori.

"Are you okay with this?" Paige asked Tori who blinked in surprise.

"No." Tori answered. "I am NOT okay with leaving Dean there to be tortured for two months." Sari tensed, she knew this was the only way they were going to be able to save Dean without sacrificing what remained of the people of Everidge. "But, we won't be any good to Dean dead either. I trust Sari." Tori look up apologetically at Paige. She seemed to think about what Tori said for a moment.

"Then I want to come with you. I want to help bring him back," Paige demanded.

"Fine." Sari agreed a little defeated. She would rather Paige stay out of the violence, but she would get nowhere fighting with her. It occurred to her then that Paige was familiar with the foliage. She assisted Millie all the time with the herbal concoctions far more than

Sari ever had.

"Paige, are they any plants here in the village that are poisonous to the Caligo?" Paige was surprised by the question.

"Well yeah, the sunflowers for starters. And there are a few others, I think."

"Meet me at Millie's tonight with a list of all of them and what they do. I have an idea!"

CHAPTER TWENTY-FOUR

Tori

Days pass slowly when you're waiting for war.

Tori tried to keep busy practicing her archery skills, but she found herself at the end of each day marking it off on a crude calendar in her house. Seth had started teaching her close combat fighting with knives, before long she could toss Seth to the ground, knife to his throat with minimal effort. It was crazy to think not long ago she was a scared little girl running from her ex-boyfriend. The thought made her laugh now, if she were to meet Beau on the sidewalk back home today, it would turn out a lot different. The thought gave her immense satisfaction and pride.

She and Seth spent every afternoon together practicing in the gully. Sometimes Allen joined them, though he had a hard time with how much better Tori was than him at, well, everything. She still tingled at Seth's touch and his lips against hers, but she tried to stay focused on the end game: rescuing Dean. They also spent every evening together, snuggling near the fire doing nothing at all. He would greet her the next day with a "Hey beautiful," and they would do it all over again.

Tori had never been happier. And stronger. She was changing.

Over time she began to notice Sari's presence less and less in the gully sparring or shooting her bow, and she also noticed a growing tension between Sari and Seth that made Tori uneasy. She had an increasing paranoia that she was the cause of the tension. She would come to gully to meet Seth only to interrupt heated discussions between the twins. When Sari would see her, she would excuse herself and leave without another word. It always took Seth awhile to shake off the effects of the conversations.

Allen and Tori met every morning for breakfast beneath the pear tree and even Allen began to seem off. With Dean's rescue looming over their heads, everyone's nerves were frayed. But when Sari didn't show one morning at her usual time Allen began to fidget and bite his nails (which really irritated Tori even though she was a nail biter herself). If Sari was avoiding her, Tori would go to her. Allen was her best friend and her only real family; they had to deal with whatever was going on. Tori was going to face it head on.

After leaving Allen nervous and fidgety, she approached Sari's house and knocked harder than she meant to. When no one answered, Tori yelled for Sari through the thick wooden door. From the other side of the door she heard a moaning that sounded like Sari. Panic suddenly took over and she shoved open the door.

"Sari?! Are you okay?" Tori almost screamed. Sari lay on the floor on the far side of her cottage, blonde hair falling in her face, surrounded by soiled rags and leaning over her water basin. She looked over at Tori weakly, she was so pale. She attempted to smile at Tori but she vomited instead into the water basin. She sat back up and wiped her face motioning for Tori to shut the door.

What is going on?

Tori stepped in and shut the door behind her. She tried to ignore the smell of vomit in the room hanging like a noxious cloud. Sari started to cry, dropping her face into hands. Tori shook her head and went to her side, settling on the floor beside her.

"Let me help you," she said as she took another clean rag and wiped the sweat from Sari's forehead, pushing the hair from her face. "Are you okay? What's going on?" Tori said quietly to her.

"I'm pregnant," Sari wept. All animosity Tori may have been holding melted away. The tension she had sensed had nothing to do with her; it had been something much bigger. Tori stared at Sari. She saw no baby bump which meant she must be very newly pregnant and that meant the father had to be...

"Allen's?" Tori guessed. Sari nodded miserably. "But Sari, that's wonderful! He loves you! You are going to be a mom, Allen's going to be dad, and I'm going to be an Aunt and Seth..." Sari held up her hand to stop her.

"It doesn't work like that here, Tori." Sari readjusted herself so she was leaning back against a nearby wall looking at Tori. "We can't have babies here. We aren't from here. Mother Nature tries to keep it that way. Only the native born can reproduce here." Sari wiped her mouth again.

"But you *are* reproducing. You're pregnant!"

"No!" Sari snapped. "If I have a baby, I have to die." Sari's eyes welled with tears again, some spilled down her face as she continued. "And even if the baby survives the birth, the age regression kills the babies almost immediately."

Tori was silent.

"Is there any way to save you and the baby?"

"I don't know." Sari laid her head on her knees and began to cry. "Tori, I don't care if I die. I've lived a hundred years and the only thing I have ever wanted was to be a mother. I cannot let this baby die." Sari looked at Tori, eyes red and swollen.

"We're not going to let that happen," Tori scooted across the floor next to Sari and put and arm around her. "We'll figure it out okay?" Sari nodded wiping the tears from her cheeks. "Does Allen know?"

"No, but I've been pretty awful to him for the last few days," Sari laughed.

"Want me to help you tell him?" Tori smiled widely, almost begging Sari to *let* her help tell Allen. Sari smiled a little and nodded.

*   *   *

Allen whooped in delight and hugged Sari tightly when he heard the news, then his elation slowly turned to dread. He cried and hugged Sari tighter. Seth said nothing. After a few minutes, he turned and left without a word. After a few minutes, Tori followed him, leaving Sari and Allen to celebrate and grieve privately. She followed him into the gully and without saying anything he sat down next to a pile of arrows and started sharpening arrowheads. Tori approached quietly.

"Seth?" he didn't respond. Or even look in her direction. She sat down next to him and put her arm around his neck, he quickly jerked away. "Hey. We'll figure something out."

"There's nothing to figure out, Tori." His tone was cold and it hurt just to hear him talk to her that way. "Sari will have the baby, and they will both die just like Hannah and…" His voice trailed off.

"Who's Hannah?"

"She came here about 15 years or so after us, we were close…." He shrugged. "She was great but nothing like this," he indicated between the two of them. "None of us had any idea what would happen when she got pregnant, then when the baby came." Seth voice choked with emotion.

"He took one tiny breath…," Seth sighed haggardly. "And then they were both gone." He continued to methodically sharpen the arrows from one pile and dropped them into another. "I've been here 40 years, and only been involved with one woman and I was okay with that…. Until I saw you at the Portis that day. You woke up what that day had killed." Seth stopped sharpening and looked at her, "I can't go through that again."

"That isn't going to happen Seth…" Tori began.

"You don't know that love! Look what happened to Sari. Whatever this is, we need to end it. Eventually you're going to go home or die and I can't take that." Seth turned back to the arrowheads, anger flushing Tori's face.

"So you're just going to shut down? Is that it?" Tori laughed, in anger. "You can still be there for your sister and… enjoy 'whatever this is,'" she said, throwing his own words back at him.

"Sorry, love," was all he said. Tori stood infuriated.

"You're a coward." She said coldly, "I'm going to try to help Allen and Sari, but by all means you sit here and feel sorry for yourself!" She turned to storm off but wasn't done. She wanted to deal the final blow. "You know, at least when Beau beat me, he faced me when he did it." Seth flinched from her words but never spoke. Tori left him there in the gully, tears stinging her eyes and her heart ripping in two.

*   *   *

As the blood moon drew closer, it was decided that, in her condition, Sari couldn't help them rescue Dean. But she insisted on accompanying them to the base of the mountain. Tori was, surprisingly, the next best archer, so she would take Sari's place. The rescue team was small, consisting only of Tori, Roth, Dru, Annie and Seth. Allen had decided he would stay with Sari and no one protested.

They plotted their course on a map spread across Millie's table. The plan was for Tori and Seth to veer off from the rest of the group and climb to a ridge across from the ceremonial mesa where they could provide cover as the rest made their way up the mountain, surprising the Caligo during their Blood Moon Ceremony.

"We're going to be outnumbered." Roth said discouraged.

Paige quickly produced a bucket of foul smelling liquid in pouches made of thin animal hide.

"Not with this we're not!" She announced proudly.

"What IS that?" Dru asked covering his nose with his work rag that he seemed to always have in his pocket.

"This is sunflower oil," Paige explained. "Boiled down and highly concentrated. It's going to be like throwing acid balloons at them."

"The Caligo use many things for medicinal purposes but one thing they NEVER used was sunflowers, that's why they stay clear of the forest. I boiled it down and Paige came up with the idea of using the shaved leather as a vessel," Millie explained, beaming with pride at Paige.

"Nice job," Sari said.

Paige smiled and then explained how the poison would work. "Once these bad boys break open, the Caligo's skin will begin to burn and boils will form and break open. Once that happens, the toxin will make its way into their blood stream and they will be dead within minutes. You'll be able to take out all the Caligo on the mesa before even entering the mountain."

"That's amazing!" Tori had to give Paige credit, this was awesome. `

"Okay, here's what we'll do," Roth began, "We'll anchor some of Paige's death balloons here to Tori and Seth's arrows, they will send them in while we make our way up on to the Mesa. We will clear the remaining Caligo and head in to get Dean. Seth and Tori, I want you on the ridge in case something happens and we need cover quick." Tori nodded but she had another plan.

"We leave at dusk."

Tori hung back and let the others file out of Millie's tiny cottage. Seth seemed to linger, waiting for her but she eventually waited him out and he left. Even Paige seemed to sense she was waiting for time with Millie and she slipped out the door. Once everyone was gone and only she and Millie remained, Tori unrolled the map again on the table.

"I need you to show me where the alchemist kept the Dragon Tears," Tori slid the map toward Millie. "Please," Millie nodded.

"The Dragon Tears aren't kept in the alchemists' lab, Lucius keeps them on him," Millie drew the route on the map as she spoke. "This is the way to Lucius' chamber. But the Dragon Tears are actually mined in the mountain like the iron. They grind it down and that's how they get the liquid form. If you can't get to Lucius, the bright blue stones are the next best thing. They will be in the mines." Tori nodded, rolling up the map and stowing it in her quiver. Millie took her hand. "Good luck, love." Tori looked down and found a small container of sunflower oil Millie had slipped in her hand. A little extra insurance never hurt. Tori hugged Millie tight and left the cottage.

Outside, in the dying sunlight, Sari and Allen sat huddled together, arms intertwined. Allen looked up when he saw her exit the cottage. He rose, leaving Sari in the shade of the tree and coming over to her.

"I can tell you're thinking about doing something stupid T-bird," Allen said quietly. Tori didn't respond, she didn't know how to. "I can't lose them."

"I know, Allen," She said softly.

"I would love to tell you to not do whatever you're planning on doing… but I can't."

"I know," Tori hugged Allen tight. "Keep Sari safe. I have a plan." Allen hugged her back before she broke away and headed toward the gully.

Dean had been a captive for over two months now. Who knew what they would find when they did rescue him, but that didn't daunt her. Sari and the baby's lives hung in the balance. She couldn't panic and couldn't run this time. It was time for her to finally, be brave.

CHAPTER TWENTY-FIVE

Dean

Days and nights blurred.

Pain and darkness became all he knew.

Beau fed enough him to keep him alive but even that food tasted tainted and dirty.

His burned leg was numb now, the wound has festered beyond retrieval and he could smell the rotting flesh. But that was the least of his worries. His body was covered in open wounds and gaping gashes. Dried blood caked his hair to his scalp and over his eyes. Three fingers were broken and his shoulders were in danger of coming out of their sockets, but he didn't care. He didn't care about any of it anymore. His mind was breaking. He had no clue how long he had been there but he didn't know how much longer he could hold on.

He thought about it every second he was conscious and dreamt about it when he passed out from exhaustion. Just letting go. But still he remained.

"I can't do it anymore," he said to the empty room. "Just let me die, please."

The silence mocked him.

Then, from out of the darkness of his mind came a song. A song he'd heard before.

"The primrose in the sheltered nook
The crystal stream the babbling brook
All these things God's hands have made for the love of
thee."

"Paige?" Dean asked the darkness.

"Twilight and shadows fall
Peace to his children all
Angels are guarding and they watch o'er thee
As you sleep
May angels watch over and may they guard o'er thee,"
Paige's ghost voice sang.

"I can't, I can't!" Dean cried.

"They are coming for you. Just hang on a little longer."

CHAPTER TWENTY-SIX

Tori

The slow walk to the mountain was torturous and had Tori's nerves on high alert. Sari and Allen left then at the base of mountain just as the blood moon made its appearance in the sky. The ridge loomed over them. Seth and Tori split from the group and positioned themselves on the crest across from the ridge. They could see Roth, Dru and Annie making their way up the cliffs. Tori mentally mapped her route for once Roth and the others had cleared the ceremonial ridge. Seth eyed her curiously but said nothing. It still hurt to look at him, it was excruciating actually. Electricity still sizzled up her skin whenever he got close to her, but she had to push that aside. She had to focus, for Dean's sake and for the sake of Sari and the baby. Seth began taking the small sacks of sunflower oil from his satchel and attaching them to the end of counter weighted arrows.

"We wait for Roth's signal," Seth whispered.

"I know the plan," Tori snapped.

"Tori... I'm sorry... I-"

"Don't!" Tori hissed. "Don't apologize for being something you're obviously not. Besides, I have bigger stuff to worry about tonight."

Seth said nothing more.

As the blood moon took its position in the night sky, the mountain opened. A great hole opened releasing a flood of enormous beings, human in form. They were clad in bones and animal hide. They formed a circle on the ridge, raising their hands high in genuflection to the blood moon.

This is it.

Be brave Tori.

Tori's heart beat furiously against her chest but she steadied her hands and readied an arrow.

"Wait for Roth," Seth whispered.

"Shut up!" Tori snarled back.

From below the ridge they saw Roth's hand wave the signal and they both released the poison arrows. The arrows flew silently across the valley, arcing up silhouetted by the moon. Tori's arrow hit first, a little left of the entrance but a good shot just the same. A fine cloud rose from the ground where the arrow had hit.

The celebrating Caligo did not take notice at first, but by the time Seth's arrow landed the first monstrous man was already wailing in pain. One after the other, reseating arrows as soon as they let the previous one fly, they unleashed their assault, blocking the entrance back into the mountain. As the sacks broke open against the rock, the massive figures began falling to the ground writhing in pain. Their screams echoed off the mountain.

Seth fired the last arrow then waved the signal for Roth and the others to storm the ridge and into the cave. By the time he looked back Tori was already gone, grabbing her bow and quiver she jumped from the crest onto the mountainside below and started toward the ridge.

"TORI!" Seth yelled from behind her.

Tori tripped and slid down the mountainside, then bounded up the ridge joining Roth, Dru and Annie. She looked around the ridge at the dead Caligo scattered around her. Their skin was blistered and bleeding, faces twisted in pain. The few that still twitched and groaned Annie and Roth disposed of.

"What are you doing here?! You're supposed to be on the ridge!" Roth demanded.

"I have to get something," Tori said quickly but Roth didn't budge. "Roth I am going in there." When Roth didn't move, Tori armed her bow and pointed it at him. Roth stepped aside. Tori lowered her bow, "It's for Sari, Roth." He sighed.

"Get what you need to get and then get the hell out," Roth instructed to Tori. "We go after Dean."

A crunch of gravel came from behind them, they all spun, weapons ready as Seth appeared over the edge of the ridge breathing hard. They all exhaled in relief.

"Do either one of you follow orders?" Roth asked

irritated. He shook his head and led them into the cave.

"Oh my god…," Dru whispered.

The cave was long, winding into the depths of the mountain and lit by torchlight. Lining the walls and the ceiling of the passage were human skulls. The bones of the jaws or forehead did not protrude like in the Caligo. The glinting of the torchlight off the bones seemed to go on forever. Roth took a deep breath then entered with Dru and Annie close behind.

"Let's go," Seth said stoically, standing aside to let her go first.

They made their way as group down the skull lined corridor. The empty eyes of the skulls seem to follow them as they walked down the passage. As they turned the corner a lone Caligo ranger, just as shocked to see them as they were him, unsheathed his sword and ran at them. Tori released an arrow which went just over his left shoulder, Roth went low with his own sword and caught the massive man in the abdomen and Annie finished him off with her knife. The man's eyes bugged and his jutting jaw moved to gulp air that would not come. Finally, he fell to his knees, then face first to the ground.

They came to a Y in the passage; Tori consulted the map Millie had given her which showed she needed to go right. Roth, Dru and Annie needed to head left to the dungeons.

"Meet us outside. Get whatever you came for and leave, got it?" Roth whispered.

"Got it." Tori confirmed. "Roth…. Please get Dean out of there." Roth nodded to Tori and took Seth by the soldier.

"You two be careful." With that he turned and the trio headed down the left tunnel into the darkness.

Seth and Tori continued down the skull lined passage, twisting further and further into the earth. The skulls went on forever.

"They've killed so many," Tori said solemnly.

They finally came to the large stone door Millie had described as "Death's Door" at the end of a dark passage. They approached the door carefully and Seth listened at it for a moment before pushing it open. They entered the dimly lit chamber of the beast. The walls were all stone, decorated with more skulls and human body parts. The room reeked of death. Tori scanned the room and saw a shelf of vials on the opposite wall, she headed for them hastily. Seth hissed at her impatiently. Tori was almost to the shelves when she saw the movement in the shadows. She froze in horror as the massive monster stepped into the light.

"I knew you would come." His voice was so deep it shook Tori to the core. "I said I would have you." Trembling from head to toe, she raised her bow.

"We need the Dragon Tears. We've already killed your army with our own poison fog, give us the Dragon Tears and we won't take any more of your men." Tori's voice sounded small but steady. Lucius roared with laughter. Tori felt each laugh thump through her like a concussive sound wave.

"You want to live forever little one?" He took a step toward Tori and Seth raised his bow from behind her.

"Not another step," Seth said. Lucius smiled but did not advance.

"Little girl's got some fight in her now, huh?" The sound of his voice made her blood run cold. In the events of the last two months she had forgotten, foolishly, about Beau. She turned towards the sound of his voice; he had come in the door behind Seth, effectively blocking them in. When she saw Beau, the air was knocked out of her. He was just as big as Lucius and just as menacing.

"What happened to you?" Tori gasped.

"This place happened!" He yelled excitedly, "This was me all along, baby girl, Lucius here just helped me unleash it!" Beau and Lucius began circling them like prey. Seth and Tori stood back to back, each with their bow raised and ready, turning as their enemies did to keep them in view.

"Just a little drink of one of those little potions there and *POOF* Badass Beau!" He smiled at her, revealing his serrated teeth.

"Beau has proven quite useful," Lucius rumbled. "But enough of this! Do what you want with her but the boy is mine." Lucius sneered. "I'm hungry."

"Tori….." Seth said, fear on the edge of his voice. "I love you." He released his first arrow at Lucius, then dropped his bow and pulled his hatchet from his waistband and brought it down as Lucius tackled him and engulfed him in his shear mass.

Beau dove for Tori but she was ready and surging with anger. She released her arrow catching Beau in the hip, his momentum knocking her off her feet. She frantically reached for her knife, slamming it into him. Beau howled in pain and Tori scurried from underneath him.

Tori scanned the room for Seth and found him just as he brought the hatchet down in Lucius's thigh. Tori ran for her bow, snatched it from the ground as she slid to her knees. She frantically uncapped the sunflower oil Millie had given her, she thrust her last arrow into the oil and seated it. Beau was on his hands and knees but before he could lunge at her again… ever again… she released the arrow.

The poison hit him straight in the chest, his face turned black and his skin bubbled and dripped. He gurgled and clawed at the air but Tori never took her eyes away from his. She wanted to see HIS fear for once.

"TORI!" Seth screamed a second too late as Lucius barreled into her, knocking the breath from her as an explosion of pain echoed through her body. She hit hard against the rock wall of the cave, making her vision double and go dark for a moment.

Her back was against the cold stone as Lucius came for her again. She pushed her legs straight out in front of her catching Lucius at the chest and holding him at leg's length, his weight crushing against her legs.

His face was within inches of hers; he gnashed his teeth at her and ripped at her with his claws. She groped desperately for a knife or the rest of the oil but could only make one of her arms obey. Her other arm was limp at her side. Lucius's weight was becoming too much for her, her knees threatened to buckle.

"NO!" she screamed. She would NOT die this way! Not now! She summoned every ounce of strength and pushed the massive beast off of her sending him reeling backward a couple feet.

He righted himself quickly as she spotted the container of sunflower oil a few feet away, stretching for it. But she didn't have time. Lucius was already on top of her again, with teeth and claws bared. She braced herself for the attack when suddenly Lucius seized and he fell lifeless to the side, hatchet sticking out of the back of his skull. Seth stood panting over him, bloody and beaten.

"Are you okay?" Seth asked. Tori nodded as she pushed the lifeless body off of her legs. She held her arm to her chest as Seth helped her up off the floor. They appraised the carnage around them.

"Here, you dropped this," Seth handed Tori her knife. "Let's get..." Seth's body went suddenly rigid, all the color draining from his face.

"Seth?" Tori said confused, "Seth?!" she cried again as Seth dropped to his knees to reveal an arrow sticking out from his back. Tori looked up and saw one of the Caligo standing in the doorway, bow still raised. Before he could even flinch she threw knife, hitting him and killing him instantly.

Seth fell forward onto the ground, gasping for breath. Tori dropped to the ground next to him and turned him on his side breaking the arrow shaft off.

"Seth.... Seth no... Please..." She pulled Seth onto her lap. "You can't leave me."

"You... gotta... get.... out...." Seth rasped before he slipped away. Tori felt the life leave his body.

"NO!" She screamed, tears streaming down her

cheeks. The she spotted the vial of blue liquid around Lucius's neck. She laid Seth gently on the ground then scrambled over to the huge corpse and ripped the chain from his neck. She crawled back over to Seth, then looked down at the small vial of Dragon Tear in her hands. She couldn't let Seth die… Not when she could save him.

"I'm sorry Allen. I'm sorry Sari." She whispered as she opened the vial and poured the gel into Seth's mouth.

Nothing happened at first. After several agonizing minutes Seth gasped in a huge breath, coughing and gagging for air. Then he opened his eyes. He focused on Tori and saw the empty vial in her hand.

"What did you do?"

"I had to…" She cried, "I love you." Tori sobbed, realizing that saving the baby and Sari was almost impossible now. Seth put his hand on the back of her head and brought her head to his chest.

"I love you, too."

*   *   *

They found Roth, Dru and Annie no worse for wear on the ridge. Tori scanned the darkness until she found him.

"Dean!" They had wrapped him in a cloak Tori could see his eye was swollen shut, and the blood caked in his hair. His emaciated frame stuck out in sharp angles from beneath the cloak. He didn't seem to know where he was, Roth had to lead him down the mountain. They had also managed to rescue four other villagers from the dungeons, they were all sickly thin but none had been tortured as badly as Dean. They headed slowly down the mountainside; Tori helped Seth limp down the cliffs and back to the forest where Allen and Sari waited anxiously.

Allen looked to Tori asking without words if she had succeeded, she only shook her head.

*   *   *

Once back in the safety of the village Millie worked for over a day to remove the arrowhead from Seth's spine. The Dragon Tears were helping Seth heal and he would be up and around in a few days. Millie also set Tori's arm and fashioned a splint from fabric and a piece of wood from a pear tree. They settled the rescued villagers in a larger cottage together until they were healthy and comfortable enough to move out on their own. But Dean refused to sleep. Millie had done what she could for his body, many scars remained, but his mind was still broken.

"I can't heal that," she had said sadly.

When his body would finally succumb to exhaustion, his screams could be heard throughout the entire village. He was quiet and withdrawn. He would have flashbacks nearly every day and begin to scream and fight against an unseen assailant.

Tori watched him from afar, but she wasn't the only one.

"He isn't the same," Tori said breaking the silence between them.

"Who would be?" Paige replied quietly. Tori Sighed heavily. "We were never meant to be together. I confused chivalry with affection. And that isn't healthy or fair to either of us. He needs someone who can *help* him now, he needs you. He's always needed you Paige." Paige stared at her for a long time, saying nothing. "Roth told me he was talking to you when they found him. He said you were singing to him," Tori smiled. "I think the thought of you was the only thing that kept him alive. Go save him now." Paige smiled in return, finally letting a peace come between the two of them. She nodded and then quietly crossed the clearing to where Dean sat. Tori watched Dean look up at her as if he were seeing an angel. He wrapped his arms around her waist and embraced her and she cradled his head in her hands.

Tori stood and left them alone to the sound of Paige's singing.

CHAPTER TWENTY-SEVEN

Seth

Seth's back still ached from the arrow wound. It had been months but he still felt the ghost of the arrow in his back. It was a reminder of a love he almost threw away.

The morning light assaulted his sleeping face, he rolled over and found Tori curled up next to him on top of the covers. He rolled onto his side next to her, careful not to wake her and just watched her for a long time. He carefully pushed a piece of her long, auburn hair over her shoulder, which he kissed softly. Her eyes fluttered then opened, looking sleepily over at him.

"Hey," she said rubbing the sleep out of her eyes, "How are you feeling?"

He couldn't take his eyes off of her, her amber eyes drew him in and he couldn't even find the worlds to speak. He leaned in and kissed her, pulling her to him as she slid under the blankets with him. He wasn't afraid anymore of what would happen tomorrow or even in a year, she was here now with him.

And then his vision blurred and all he saw was blue.

"Seth? Seth!" Tori was over him calling his name when he came to. He was still in bed next to Tori but they were no longer in a loving embrace and Tori's face was lined with fear. "Are you okay?"

"I'm fine," Seth said, Millie had warned him that when the visions started they would be intense and when he least expected... He wasn't ready for that. "The Portis is opening. I saw it." Tori's face lit up.

"We can go home?" She said excitedly, and then her face darkened. "We can go home...," she said solemnly. Seth stroked her cheek reassuringly.

"We need to get the others, yeah?" Seth said.

"Yeah," Tori kissed him once more before going to find the others.

CHAPTER TWENTY-EIGHT

Tori

She couldn't leave.

She had to leave.

She wouldn't leave.

She had to leave.

Tori argued with herself the entire way to the cottage Allen and Sari now shared. They had decided two cabins were silly once Sari really started to show, and when you don't know how long you have with someone… Well everything seemed silly.

When she reached the cottage she heard Sari screaming in pain, without thinking she drew her knife and busted into the cottage. Allen's terrified face greeted her.

"Tori! Sari's water just broke! Help me!" Allen said frantically, holding Sari close on the bed.

"What? Isn't it too soon?" Tori cried putting her knife away. "Oh my god, the Portis! Allen we have to get her to the Portis! It's open!" She ran to Sari's side and as they each took and arm, they lifted her up off the bed. "If we get her through before the baby comes, maybe they will both survive."

Sari screamed in pain again as they came into the village. Seth came running over panic written all over his face.

"Seth, I need you to go get Dean and Paige," Seth was frozen in fear watching his sister, "Seth!" Tori yelled. He looked at her. "Go get Dean and Paige."

*   *   *

They made their way to back through the forest and to the field where Portis glowed brightly. The more intense Sari's contractions got, the slower they had to go. Seth and Dean helped carry her the last 100 yards to the stone.

"She doesn't have much time," Seth said.

"We don't even know if this is going to work," Sari cried.

"You have to try!" Seth hugged his sister fiercely then looked at Allen, "Take care of her!" Allen nodded scooping Sari up in both his arms and going to the stone. Dean followed, hand trailed back in Paige's grasp.

"You too!" Tori screamed over the noise over the stone at Paige. "Go!" Paige ran to the stone with Dean as the pulses got fasted and more intense.

"Tori! We have to go!" Allen screamed at her. Tori jumped into Seth's arms and kissed him, arms wrapped tightly around his neck.

"I love you!" She shouted. The light grew brighter from the stone and Dean was pulled against it with Paige.

"Tori go, or you won't be able to," Seth said letting her go. She turned and walked toward the bright blue stone. Allen, with Sari still in his arms was pulled hard against the stone as the pulses grew faster.

"Tori, come on!" Allen yelled for her. Then he saw the look in her eyes. "Tori! NO!"

In a wave of blinding blue light, they were gone.

CHAPTER TWENTY-NINE

Allen

When he woke, he immediately looked around the field for Tori, but she was nowhere to be found.

"Allen?" he turned to see Sari curled on her side a few feet from him. He crawled to her quickly and as he neared he saw HER.

In Sari's arms, swaddled in her cloak, was his baby girl. Allen collapsed against Sari, as they both cried tears of joy. Dean and Paige found them and Paige fell to her knees when she saw Sari and the baby.

Allen leaned down and kissed his blue-eyed baby girl.

Victoria.

EPILOGUE

She only needed a second to decide.

Tori turned away from the Portis and its blue light and ran back to Seth's arms.

The Portis would open again. There would be more chances to get home, if she ever wanted to go home.

The Caligo were not done and they would want revenge for killing Lucius. And that was okay. They had something she wanted too, the only supply of Dragon Tears.

So she would help defend this tiny village against them. She wasn't the same girl who had come through that stone doorway. Seth had helped her become this new, braver version of herself. She had no idea what tomorrow held, but she knew now she wasn't afraid. She knew she was strong. She knew could face tomorrow.

The Ballyeamon Cradle Song

Rest tired eyes a while
Sweet is thy baby's smile
Angels are guarding and they watch o'er thee.

Sleep, sleep, grah mo chree *
Here on you mamma's knee
Angels are guarding
And they watch o'er thee.

The birdeens sing a fluting song
They sing to thee the whole day long
Wee fairies dance o'er hill and dale
For very love of thee.

Dream, Dream, grah mo chree
Here on your Mamma's knee
Angels are guarding and they watch o'er thee
As you sleep may Angels watch over
And may they guard o'er thee.

The primrose in the sheltered nook
The crystal stream the babbling brook
All these things God's hands have made
For very love of thee.

Twilight and shadows fall
Peace to His children all

Angels are guarding and they watch o'er thee

As you sleep

May Angels watch over and May the guard o'er thee.

* grah mo chree is Gaelic for "sweetheart".

The Ballyeamon Cradle Song is an Irish lullaby that was recovered from an old song book by Aine Ui Cheallaigh.

CPSIA information can be obtained
at www.ICGtesting.com
Printed in the USA
LVHW032229070622
720606LV00014B/591

9 781940 938707